FTB PRESS PRESENTS: THE RENEGADES OF PROSE: AN ANTHOLOGY

FTB Press, LLC.

Chandler, AZ USA

Printed in the USA.

ISBN-13: 978-0692814932 (FTB Press)

ISBN-10: 0692814930

TABLE OF CONTENTS

The Psychologist by Maggie Veness   7

A Piece of Pollack by Jessica Bowden   15

Lilah by Catherine A. MacKenzie   25

Exterminated by DJ Tyrer   35

I Pray by Essel Pratt   45

Full Moon by Lance Hyden   53

Iraqis Speak Sorani by Paul Rhodes   61

Bumps by Phil Richardson   73

Patty Hearst has a Gun by Sandi Sonnenfeld   85

Karma by Na'amah Segal   97

The Concise Life of Henry Stallworthy by Stephen McQuiggan
                                                     111

Diagnosis by Bryn Fortey   119

The Ride by Rob Nicholson   129

Carved in Stone by Frank Roger   137

Good Dog by Chris Moylan   149

The Loved Boy by Jill Boyles   159

A Definition of Evil by Mike Sherer   171

Shuffle by James Pyne   185

THE PSYCHOLOGIST

By Maggie Veness

Marcie's in the kitchen licking her thumb, sorting last night's fifties, twenties, tens, and fives into tidy piles and writing in the ledger. Everyone has their name at the top of a column in Marcie's ledger and there's a fifty-fifty split with the House. It's raining and no one has buzzed for an hour.

"Gonna be a slow night, ladies," she calls across the breakfast bar.

Marcie mostly wears crop-tops with leopard-print tights. She's experienced in every aspect of work in a House and occasionally still entertains a certain type of client—the type who takes comfort in being suckled. We don't know her exact age but she has skin like dusty crepe-paper and, the night she tripped down the back steps, both her implants exploded her breasts returned to being skinny and low-slung, which pissed her off, but she can still work those thimble-sized nipples.

Amy's our baby. Her House name's Ninette. She's nineteen but looks way younger. Her collagen-plumped pout glistens with dewy-pink lip gloss and when she blinks, her golden fringe bounces up and down on jet-black eyelash extensions. Amy has the Baby-Doll look: a genuine Daddy-trap. Little thing can make a grand in one night when the Daddies come to town for some convention. I've been watching her from my favorite club chair in the corner. Mesmerized by an ancient episode of M.A.S.H., she hasn't said a word since she arrived for work. She's perched in the center of our new paisley-print sofa, knees tucked under her chin. When that sofa was delivered last Thursday afternoon we made three hundred bucks in twenty minutes entertaining the Turkish truck driver and his two sweaty muscle-men. Marcie said that sofa turned out to be a real bargain after her hundred-and-fifty cut. An entire cigarette just burned away between Amy's sculptured, cinnamon-rose fingernails. She's totally wasted and doesn't think anyone can tell.

My House name's Cassandra but my regulars get to call me Cassie. Mine's the Cougar look. When I started out twenty-five years back I had the Baby-Doll. I'd spent eighteen months living scared and lonely on the street. You land a job in a House and you've got yourself an instant family. These days I pay the salon for my blonde locks and summery tan, but I've got a drawer full of toys I know how to use, and when I squeeze my shapely, God-given derrière into a teensy tube-skirt I still have no problem making my rent.

Mai-Lin's here—seated at the card table in the corner wearing a pair of those tiny, frameless glasses. Every minute Mai-Lin's not working, she's studying. She arrives lugging a laptop, medical books, and her own special cushion. She gets that thick, blue-black hair of hers cut into a short-back-and-sides at the local barber shop. Mai-Lin's is the Pretty-Boy look—something that speaks particularly to men who secretly aren't attracted to women. She says having no tits or hips is good for business, but we all see how bad she needs to sit on that special donut cushion of hers between clients. Mai-Lyn's real proud about paying all her university fees up front. Eighteen months from now she'll have letters after her name and a soft, suede captain's chair to sit on. Gemma and Leanne are in the bathroom painting each other's toenails. They share the Girl-Next-Door look: not so different from your friendly neighbor or best friend's sister. They're both mid-twenties. Both single mothers. They mostly work together.

Submerged in the purple corduroy bean-bag to my right is our Denise. She's keeping her mind sharp with an intermediate level Sudoku puzzle book. Denise was Denis until twelve months back. She's so popular she only has to work two shifts each week. Denise's make-up and hair are always immaculate. Today she's wearing a fluffy, long-sleeved mauve blouse with a white, pleated mini-skirt and strappy silver platforms. Denise has the longest and best legs I've ever seen. Her look is the Italian Movie Star. Apparently, she worked around the Tranny Cabaret joints in the city for eight years, kept on saving 'til she had enough to pay a surgeon to carve off all those unwanted Denis parts. Barely four weeks after the big operation she turned up at our House, eager for us girls to check out her new sexuality. Guess it was kind of like a job interview. When she started peeling off her white, leather skirt and satin G-string we gathered like kids around an ice-cream van. Suddenly she's leaning back on the sofa, throwing her legs wide apart. She looked so happy. When we saw the thick, red stitch lines, the puckered wedges of crafted flesh, and that golf-ball sized cavity, conversation stalled.

Amy sniffed. Mai-Lyn adjusted her glasses and craned forward.

"Wow," I said.

"How amazing!" said Marcie, and rubbed her hands together.

"I know!" Denise squealed. "Anthony promised that as long as I keep up the hormone treatments, by next summer I'll have tiny titties and a perfect pussy. Anthony's my surgeon. God, and isn't he an absolute honey! I told him if I land a job here he can drop by any time he wants and I'll blow him for free."

We were all relieved to have hunky Anthony to chat about. Denise said she'd be willing to share him around so we could score free cosmetic surgery consultations. I secretly contemplated investing in some thimble-sized nipples for later on. Gemma and Leanne said they'd like tummy-tucks and would try hard to save enough cash. Not so easy when you have to pay sitters every night, but I guess they'd be paying sitters if they were out waiting on tables or stacking supermarket shelves. Anyhow, Anthony still hasn't dropped by.

Comes down to simple choice. You can try surviving on welfare or work for a living. Marcie's girls need money same as everyone else on the planet. Here, an average week's work covers the basics, like food and rent and school fees, but if a girl has a little habit, an expensive lawyer, or, like me, a pretty MG to keep on the road, she'll be looking to her private clients for some good fast cash. Right now I've got three regulars. Figured I'd need a nest egg for after the phone stops ringing, so a year back I began stashing two-fifty a week into an empty photo album. Got no relatives who want to know me and it's too late to start a proper family of my own. Had the chance with this sweet guy a few years back, but like they say, no use crying over spilt milk.

Far as private clients go, my current favorite is Doctor George. He's my easy hour from 9 p.m. each Monday. He's well-spoken and real polite, late sixties with stringy, grey hair and a face resembling the surface of the moon. Doctor George has a thing about punctuality and I've never let him down. At five to nine he slips a key under the rubber mat out front of his apartment then heads back inside to wait in his bedroom. I let myself in and flick the deadlock, place the key on the sideboard, then change into the clothes he's chosen for our appointment while he watches through a peep-hole in his door. I guess he finds my outfits at charity stores. I don't mind. They're washed and pressed and laid out ready along the back of his marine-blue, vinyl divan. It's impressive the way he gets the sizes right. Whether it's a skirt, blouse, and cardigan in shades of pink, or a tailored pantsuit with an airlines-style scarf, there's always a lacy suspender belt and seamed stockings for underneath. I take my time and put on a good show—make sure he gets a flash of the hairless mound between my legs. He waits in there 'til I call out I'm ready, Doctor.

Dr. George is stuck in a wheelchair and I'll never let on I know he's never been any sort of doctor. This ex private escort friend I often bump into at the hair salon told me she'd seen him naked plenty of times at the Repatriation Hospital. These days she works there as a massage therapist and she reckons the shrapnel he took during his third tour of Vietnam left his body looking like pink Swiss cheese. I didn't tell her about the doctor thing. I'm glad he gets a buzz outa wearing that white coat and stethoscope. Glad he can still enjoy something. In certain situations, I reckon my job is just as important as a psychologist.

Dr. George has a portable massage table set up in the lounge-room, covered with a crisp, white sheet. The second he snaps on the latex gloves his hands begin to tremble. I have to wait for his instructions, even though they're the same every week.

"Remove your panties only, please, and lie down on the table."

"Yes, Doctor."

"Pull your knees up for me. Good. Try to relax. Now drop them wide apart and prepare yourself for an internal examination."

"Yes, Doctor."

Once I'm in position Dr. George carefully pegs my generous external parts aside, slowly inserts a pair of those metal duck-bill things, then uses a tiny silver torch to peer inside. He has this expensive-looking gold pen and black leather clip-board. During my examination, he scribbles endless notes, pausing now and then to tap the pen against his forehead and stare at the ceiling. His writing looks like miniature hieroglyphics.

When he's done exploring he hands me a large specimen jar and sends me to the bathroom. I hear him wheel up outside the door to listen while I pee. He likes me to fill the jar to the top and leave it on the bathroom vanity. I guess there's a peep-hole somewhere in that door as well. Best not to think about what he does with my pee after I'm gone.

I come out and straddle his chair; rub my shaven parts over his sleeping crotch for a bit, then fake a screamer. I get that he wants the neighbors to hear. By this time he's smiling and his face and neck are blotchy-red. I tell him I can't get off with anyone else. By the time he sees me out he's looking way more relaxed and confident. See what I mean about the psychologist thing?

Dr. George is nice enough, but even without the chair he wouldn't be my type. Anyway, a client isn't someone you should ever fall for. It almost happened to me once. Name was Ray. He was slim and tall with curly, fair hair and this silky voice and these brown, puppy-dog eyes that crinkled up when he smiled. That was a few years back but now and then I still think I see him walking way ahead of me in a crowded mall, or like the other day, seated alone at a sidewalk café while I crawled by in my soft-top at peak hour. My hand flew to the horn, but then I kinda froze.

The door buzzer sounds and I realize it's stopped raining. We all jump up and follow Marcie into the foyer. While she talks prices at the door we line up and tidy ourselves.

She shows in a guy around fifty and he rests his damp umbrella in the plastic tray beside the door. He's wearing a tailored charcoal suit, yellow silk tie, and expensive cologne. His shoes are shinier than Amy's pout. Definitely not from 'round here. As Marcie introduces each of us we give him our best you-won't-regret-choosing-me smile, but its Denise's long legs that catch his eye. He nods in her direction. She steps forward and takes his hand, leads him into the Lavender Room and closes the door. We return to our favorite places in the lounge-room and I fall straight back to thinking about sweet Ray.

He came to the House a dozen times within three weeks and chose me every time. And then, this one night, the moment I close the bedroom door, Ray takes my hands and tells me he loves me; says he wants me to quit the House because I'm too special and too beautiful to share; says he wants to take me up to Willow Tree Creek to meet his mother, quit his job at the bank and build us a timber cabin down by the willows. Ray always was gentle and well mannered, but on this night he worked even harder at taking his weight on his elbows and knees. Those puppy-eyes never left my face. Then, in that few seconds after a man blows but before he falls asleep on top of you, Ray asks me to marry him. I don't know what to say so I just say I'll definitely think it over. Then he's asleep and I have actual tears rolling down my cheeks.

I let him stay there for a few extra minutes breathing deep and peaceful while I looked around at the stack of towels on the dresser near the wash-basin and the mini safe in the wall and the panic button beside the bed and the pretty glass dish with assorted condoms, and I knew if I went to Willow Tree Creek with Ray that room would be where my mind flew back to every time his breath slowed like that against my neck.

A PIECE OF POLLOCK

By Jessica Bowden

Well, where to begin? I guess I should tell you that I'm an artist, and as an artist, I'm not exactly starving, but gut-bustingly full doesn't quite express my condition either. And yes, it is a condition. Can you imagine waking up at any given hour of the day with the absolute need to spill your madness onto a canvas? Being haunted by images that roll through your mind like Van Gogh's swirling clouds in a starry night? Well…I hope not, for your own sanity, anyway.

It is exactly this condition that got me into this situation in the first place. Having recent luck selling a few paintings through local vendors and coffee shops, one of the city's galleries offered me a quaint spot as a locally featured artist. I'd get all the glitz and glam of soft incandescent lighting and a little plaque to bear my name along with a brief description of my "style" and "influences." I'm not sure when chaos became a style or insanity became an influence worth mentioning, but I felt compelled all the same to describe myself as someone obsessed with nihilistic absurdity that vomited the abjection of the human condition. Ah, yes…another condition. Needless to say, the gallery classified me as a "Postmodernist" invested in the works of Pollock and some other guy I've never even heard of.

You know, I've always been struck by that: the need for artists to classify each other. To put one another into nice neat categories of prescribed meaning. That's not life—that is not how life works! At least not my life. It's like the headline in the newspaper this morning: "Recent car crash victim charged in connection to murder case." Both a victim and a perp! That's what we all are.

So anyway, I get this invite to a stuffy party with all of those "art types." A bunch of yuppies with nothing better to do than pretend they know shit about shit, and I decided to go…dateless. This was, of course, my first mistake. Set myself up to be taken by her. Should have gone with that rocker chick from the bar; she wouldn't have let things get so out of control.

I wandered into this house, well it wasn't really a house; it was more like a manor. There were high ceilings and absolutely everything was made of wood. I couldn't help but think about insurance. Insurance for my concrete condo was through the roof. This place was one matchstick away from complete annihilation. I wondered whether "full of wood" and "dryer than a nun's cunt" was on the insurance application to describe the home's interior. Surely, insurance companies must account for the laws of probability?

I was greeted immediately (as was expected) by the owner of the estate, "Welcome, welcome. We're so glad you could make it. Your work is making quite the little splash in our circles."

This man was awful. He smelled of the bourbon once housed in his rock glass and stood no taller than five feet. His thin moustache was what put him over the edge. I was just waiting for him to stroke it as he snarled about the leftist occupiers that couldn't leave industry to the industrious.

His wife, or the woman I assumed to be the person he shared residence with, wandered over and with an equally disingenuous arm outstretched to "meet my acquaintance." I responded by saying I was "charmed" with what I hoped to be a passable amount of pretense to feel less like a fish out of water.

I, "absolutely had to try the champagne," as it was, "to die for," and I will admit, it was unlike the Spumante Bambino I was used to. The bubbles raced to my head and I felt as though I could almost cough up a conversation with one of these people who, "so very much enjoyed my work."

I sat down on the couch with a bit of a thud, having assumed the leather cushions to be softer than they were. Then I saw her. She sat facing the center of the room with her legs tucked so tightly together I wanted to tell her to, "Let it breathe." Her blonde hair was positioned just right in the bob-style of the late 1920s and her earrings dangled down below her shoulders. I couldn't help but stare. She turned when a roar of laughter burst behind me and I caught her eye. She looked up with that, "I'm going downtown," look in her eyes, and smiled at me almost coyly. I couldn't help but feel a slight rush of excitement, and imaged taking her behind one of the oversized bookshelves. I'm certain she purred like a pussy cat but I liked to imagine she was much wilder, letting me tear off her panties and shove her face into the hardcover section that made up most of the shelves.

She stood up in her white gown that looked like an opal ring my grandmother used to wear and replaced herself at my side.

"Hello," she said so calmly that I knew she couldn't read my thoughts.

"Hi," I said, shifting my arm over to the inside of my right leg.

"Nice party."

I nodded slightly and after an awkward minute she continued.

"So you don't come to these kinds of soirées often, huh?"

The change in her tone made me laugh, "No." I responded honestly. She had confirmed my feelings of unease; I stuck out like a sore thumb. Maybe it was my second hand suit or the paint splatter on the inside of my left shoe, although I was quite certain it was neither. My discomfort, my unruly sense of self, my condition, could be read a mile away. A social misfit that belonged neither to the simple folk nor to the elite; I was stuck in a maddening state of limbo, somewhere between absolute love and absolute…violence.

Just then I noticed a rather portly, unctuous man standing in the doorway. "Ah," he said, "there is something rather ubiquitous about this place."

What a prick. I could swear I could hear him breathing through his hair-stuffed nostrils from across the room.

He entered and walked around slowly. As if smelling out a mystery object like a police dog, he meticulously poked at his all-too-familiar surroundings, looking for that one thing that was out of place.

He finally stopped in front of the mantle and identified that which had been driving his canine instincts: a miniature, gold plated rearing horse.

"Here it is! Yes, I knew there was something that gave me that uncanny sense of déjà vu when I walked into this room."

"Ah, yes, of course! You've seen my cheval d'or before! Precious creature! It was recently featured in Art and Antiques Magazine," said the man with the moustache whose upper lip seemed to twitch with pleasure at the recognition.

"Yes, yes. I did see it featured. I did, however, see it long before it came into your possession. An antique dealer friend of mine once had it as a part of his personal collection. Unfortunately, when the wife found out about the extra time he was spending with his assistant, Roberto, his collection and entire life had to be downsized."

The room set into a laughter like I've never heard. There was an air in their throats that seemed to keep them from actually letting out a sound that resembled true laughter—it was more as if they were choking on their own life force. The quintessence inside of them was trying to escape through their mouths just to get caught in their esophagus and sent back down to the pits of their stomachs.

I couldn't take it anymore. In that moment my condition compelled me to grab the unnamed woman by my side and make for the door.

She seemed surprised but not entirely hesitant. I took that as a good sign and continued to make my way across the room, hoping that Mr. Moustache would get the hint and fetch us our jackets.

"Leaving already?" Mrs. Moustache said with a surprised expression on her face that made her look as though she had just learned of the recent passing of her beloved kitty, Miss Moustache.

I replied with a firm, "Yes," took our jackets from our host's arms and flung open the door without giving the white-dress-wearing-coy-eyed-bookshelf-blasted-lady a chance to get her coat wrapped around her bare arms.

And this brings me to my current situation. I'm sitting here my car with Jane Doe and I cannot for the life of me figure out what to do with her. One half of me wants to embrace her and spew my cockles all over her white dress and the other half of me wants to bash her head in for smelling me out so easily.

"So," she said, half smiling. "You've got me here; now what are you going to do with me?"

The question is too much for me to handle and instead of answering, I let out a loud grunt.

She seems startled and moves uncomfortably in the passenger seat, gesturing somewhat at the door handle.

She pauses to take another look at me. I can only hope that her hesitance to leave isn't founded on some need to get a good look at the perp that tried to kidnap her for when she called the police.

I inhale deeply and let my breath out slow. "I want to show you my place," a voice from somewhere inside of me says. The voice is so unfamiliar that I am certain someone else must be in the car with us. I look around with what has become a paranoid habit of mine, letting my eyes dart around the space uncontrollably.

She smiles again with her perfectly stained lips and bleached teeth, and grabs me by the hand. I don't know what this bitch wants or what the fuck she's doing in this car with me, but I can't wait another second and have her change her mind. I hope she's just a slut but maybe this is her idea of a joke. Good one!

I start up the car and the engine of my '96 Corolla sputters as if yelling at the guests inside to come out for another "laugh." I peel off from the boulevard unable to control my muscles. My condition worsens and my heart is racing and I can't seem to drive fast enough. In the blur of the street lights and the smeared shapes of houses a perfect image comes to mind.

The windshield becomes splattered with reds and yellows, blending and weaving, indistinct yet stark. The pavement becomes a dream that sheds sprinkles of gleaming glass into the plethora of neon-injected colours.

My eyes begin to dart once more and I feel as though I may vomit. The colours begin to permeate my corneas and enter into my head through my nose. My condition has grown worse – I know I'm close to death. The shards of glass from the road spray into my lungs through their red and yellow carriers and burn my insides as I attempt exhalation.

The next thing I know, the cat purring woman is sucking in the mixture of blended splatters with a look of terror on her face. She seems to be choking on the reds. I want to save her, but I know it's too late.

With the screeching of my tires I race into what I recognize as the entrance to the underground parking of my apartment building. As concrete as the inside, the facade of the building looks like a prison minus the bars on the windows. The glaring and blaring of the incandescent spotlights in the garage awaken me from my hallucinogenic haze. The girl still looks petrified, but the red has left her mouth, and I arrogantly ask her what her problem is.

"Nothing," she replies. "You just seemed to get lost in the race—you didn't respond to a single one of my questions."

"Yeah...I'm not really into questions." Not really "into" questions?! What does that even mean?! "I just like being in the now—I don't want to have to put life's intangibles into some narrative."

This strangely seemed to satisfy her. "Okay," she says. "No more questions." I nod and we begin to walk across the grey concrete toward the green-chipped metal storm door. Her heels click insistently and echo off of the divots in the ceiling. What am I doing here?

As we make our way through the green-grey hall to the elevator I feel dizzy again and I'm overwhelmed by the desire to take her right there. That is why she came, right? What else could she want from me?

The elevator is slow in coming and my eyes roll over the floor numbers as they light up. The tilt in my neck toward the ceiling doesn't make me feel less dizzy but I don't know where else to look. Out of my peripheral vision I can feel her staring at me and I can tell she's suppressing her laughter! Fuck you, bitch!

Her opal dress catches the florescent lighting and blinds me. I know I need to regain control, but why is she doing this to me?

"You look nervous."

You look nervous, bitch.

I finally remove my eyes from the plate above the elevator as the doors open. I walk onto the elevator before her. She hesitates. Guess I'm not a gentleman. She should have known that.

"Nah, I'm just trying to remember if I tidied up before I left."

Finally, floor 5. The doors open to more concrete and I wish she'd trip and knock her perfect teeth out. Maybe then she'd know she's not better than me.

We make out on the way down the hall to the door of my condo and I fumble with my keys. Shit, I am nervous. She moves in close to me as I place the key in the slot and turn it. When I open the door a sudden blotch of red splatters onto the wall facing the kitchen.

And then it occurs to me. She has come here to be my masterpiece.

I slam her body into the wall and moans with what I assume to be pleasure. I kiss her fuchsia rose lips and smear the sweetness to blur with her flesh-died face. She kisses me back and reaches downtown. The excitement overwhelms me and I feel the orgasm enter the base of my balls. I spill on my own fucking pants.

She gives a little laugh and retracts her palm. She did come here to laugh at me.

I'm instantly blinded by my condition and my anger unleashes hues of new sorts. Purples and reds unleash in previously unknown furies. The brown-red smells of iron and tastes sticky as it is thrust all over everything.

My walls, my sofa, my kitchen are all painted with the passion of my condition. All sounds are muted and sight is the only sense I experience until the ringing begins. With the piercing sound of running red, I am deafened and my eyes bulge out of my head with the pain. I raise my hand before my face and see that it too has been transformed by the glory of my art.

Before me, a perfect canvas lies. Every colour is in its rightful place. It almost looks like it's moving.

I can see clear as day, it stirs! And then it croaks and I come to. I stare at what I have created. It is magnificent. But will they think so? This is the painting that's compelled me my whole life. It has finally come true. I have solidified my place amongst the greats. Eat your heart out Mr. Pollock!

I rush to get my phone to take a picture. Everyone needs to see this! Where did I put it? These things are never where they're supposed to be! I throw couch pills, check all the pockets in my laundry pile, and even go so far as to check in the fridge! Wouldn't be the first time!

I eventually find it on the floor between my bed and the wall. I have a text. It's from my mom so I ignore it. I run back to other side of my condo and position myself on top of the kitchen counter. I want to make sure I get the angle just right. I snap the pic and post it to my page. I wonder who will "like" it!

I am so excited I consider going back to the party to experience a sense of superiority over those stuffy bastards. They'll never know real-life. They're heads are too far above the water to know where life stems from. I'd love one of those bloody hors d'oeuvres now! Crunch, crunch, eat shit, shit heads!

I got another text. Still mom. Are you alright? Of course I'm alright. I'm better than alright! For the first time in my life, it's as if my condition has brought me true glory!

My phone alerts again. Your recent photo has been reported and removed. What the fuck? What is happening here? Why didn't anyone "like" it? Who would report it? I'll kill that bastard! My hand starts to tremble.

My phone rings. I throw it on the couch and back away. My head fills with the toxic purgative of my condition. I feel weak.

My knees give out and a slimy yellow blinds my eyes as I vomit. I scream and hear the far off cry of sirens. They don't know art. No one does. Fucking pigs.

I curl up in a ball next to my painting extending my hand to get a feel of my genius. I hear a pounding on the door. Fuck off, fuck off, fuck off! I don't move and it continues until a cracking sound releases a cold smear of true blue floods my concrete condo. My insurance will have a field day!

LILAH

By Catherine A. Mackenzie

Lilah limped through the kitchen. She grabbed hold of the edge of the countertop to steady herself and then leaned back against the refrigerator. The scratchy shards of the rusty door chaffed into her flesh through her thin bodice, reminding her of the numerous times Zack had shoved her against the door. The cast iron frying pan often followed, the resulting dent and jagged edges adding depth and more texture to the abrasive avocado-green surface.

She massaged her right leg. The varicose veins, one in particular, ached horribly. She was aware of surgery and new-fangled laser treatments. Considered cosmetic, the cost would be prohibitive, and what doctor would deem such procedures necessary at her age?

She moaned and slid to the floor, scraping her back down the length of the fridge, but the pain in her leg overpowered any other pain. Thus, she barely felt the tear in her back or the blood seeping through the torn fabric. What was another page in an already overflowing atlas of scars amassed over the past eighty-nine years? Her mama had told her she'd received her first badge at six months when her daddy, obviously in a fit of rage, had hurled her out the window. Lilah hadn't asked why he'd do that to a defenseless babe and thanked God she'd survived her childhood years.

How many years did she have left? Notwithstanding her father's acts, she must be deserving of a reward to have endured as long as she had. But, whether the good Lord granted her two months or two years, she'd take what she could.

She crawled to the kitchen table, reached up, and guided the wicker basket to the floor. The knife glinted beside her. She'd been buttering bread when the knife slid from her greasy fingers and hit the linoleum with a slight clunk. She hadn't been able to find the knife at first. Had it taken cover behind a curl in the linoleum or slipped beneath a crack in the wooden floor? And when she located it, she hadn't had the energy to lean down to pick it up, so she had smeared the butter with her index finger.

The knife, still greasy, was cold from the drafts. The old cabin, built by her grandparents, had weathered numerous winters but hadn't received necessary upkeep. Jeremiah and their son, Zack, had let the place disintegrate into wracking ruination, and Lila hadn't been able to prevent it. Oh, she had tried. Hammer and handsaw and other tools lay in the wooden crate that served as a side table by her rocker, and an ancient toolbox of smaller items sat on the kitchen shelf. She had wielded the hammer many times, as well as the saw and pliers. Even the axe, propped against the log siding on the front porch, had been used by her, too.

But no more. The pain had been so unbearable the past couple of years that seasons had come and gone without her being able to do much other than chop firewood, which was a huge accomplishment, albeit a necessary one, for death by freezing had never appealed to her. Thanks to Tom Hodges down the road, who took pity and dumped logs on her property each fall, she'd been able to replenish the ever-dwindling woodpile. But how much longer could she hack at lumber to produce firewood? How much longer could she even stuff the old woodstove?

At least her men had ensured the cabin was warm, though they had, of course, selfish motives. Who wanted to be cold? Both of them—another pain she'd sooner forget. And for a moment, as she lay on the floor while pain overwhelmed her, she did forget. Current pain always took precedence over that of the past. In fact, one pain at a time was her motto.

But lately, she'd suffered endless pain. At her age, would it ever end?

She fingered the knife's edge. Not as sharp as she'd like, but it would have to do; she'd make it do. The grease would help. Thankfully, she'd been able to reach her basket.

She raised the bottom of her dress, revealing fleshy legs road-marked with tiny red spider veins, enlarged blue veins, and scaly patches of white and brown. A wide, protruding purple stripe on her right leg glared at her. If she could get rid of that elephantine vein, she'd be much improved. She hiked her dress farther, to the enormous blue bulb on her inner thigh. She could do it, couldn't she?

When she pressed upon the bulbous blob, it would disappear for an instant before returning, like an embarrassing blush on one's cheek. Not that she cared about appearances. Life—everything she knew—was about pain. Sighing, she glimpsed one of her quilts draped over the threadbare futon. A smile crossed her face: the delight of crafting. She had taken such care with her quilting, the precise tiny stitches attaching one fabric square to another. Of course, that had been eons ago, when she was younger and still possessed perfect eyesight, slender fingers and unwavering hands.

She reached into the basket and withdrew a pair of small fabric scissors. She'd had to hide the sewing scissors from Zack, who had never cared about utensils that served one—and only one—purpose. Specialty scissors dulled horribly if they were used on anything but fabric, but circumstances dictated she disobey one of her own steadfast rules.

After numerous tries, she succeeded in slipping the beige thread through the small eye of the needle. What else did she need? A clasp—two. She pulled hairpins from her bun and rummaged in the basket for tweezers.

And alcohol. Alcohol was a necessity. She grasped the knob of the door beneath the sink. Bottles of every size and shape and colour greeted her. She almost clapped in glee, but she wasn't a child full of joy and gaiety. Laughter didn't spew from her lips. Pain did.

She withdrew an amber-filled bottle and eyed the items on the floor—knife, tweezers, scissors, threaded needle, clasps—lined up in a neat, even row. After a great gulp of whiskey, she poured capfuls over her leg and the utensils. She swigged more of the calming liquid. Since she wasn't much of a drinker, the alcohol would hit her hard. She swiped at dribble on her chin and grimaced before thrusting the knife into the skin at her ankle, where the vein seemed to dissolve to nothing. But that was an illusion, of course. There was no end to veins, which roamed one's body relentlessly.

The excruciating pain hit her before the liquor did, but a few minutes of pain versus endless pain-filled years propelled her forward. She inserted the tweezers into the flesh, latched onto the throbbing vein, and pulled it to the surface. She attached the hairpins on the vein, precisely an inch apart. With the scissors, she made a clean cut. Grasping the needle in her bloodied fingers, she overcast the vein's edges, letting the end leading to her ankle slip back beneath the skin. The other she lay across her bloody leg.

She eyed the pulsating knob on her upper leg. She couldn't fathom digging into that mass. She'd surely bleed to death. But what did she have to lose? She held the knife two inches beyond the blue bulb and repeated the process of digging and suturing.

And then all that remained was to pull the eel-like tube from her leg. While pondering her accomplishment, she vomited twice. Two ends lay before her, both ends and incisions seeping blood. She hoped the mess looked worse than it was. Could she latch onto one end of the slimy vein and pull it through the length of her leg? And which end?

After selecting the dangling vein on her inner thigh, she wondered whether she needed to pull it through. What would happen if she let the vein sink back from whence it came? More blood seeping beneath her skin wouldn't matter, would it? Wouldn't the vessel simply wither and die, just as she would? No, she'd better drag it out.

After wiping her hands on the already bloodied skirt, she grabbed the end. The bulbous section had diminished. She figured the blood had exploded out of its casing. She pulled carefully, not knowing the durability of veins when exposed to the elements. She couldn't chance having it break midstream. Her gnarled fingers grasped more and more of the slippery thread, as if she played tug of war, pulling, over and over, revealing more vein. The pain was excruciating, but the end neared. In more ways than one.

And then she was done. She upchucked again. She fingered the slithery vein, strong yet delicate, the cause of so much grief. "Goodbye, dear vein," she muttered, and threw the spaghetti-like strand to the wall where it latched like Velcro, the end wagging like a scarecrow in a gale. Scarecrow? Lilah giggled.

Threaded needle in hand, she stitched up the two holes. Tiny, precise, neat stitches. She sipped more whiskey before pouring more over her leg. Pink fluid spread from her leg to the floor. She inhaled a stench that reminded her of men's hot breath upon her face and scouring the old cast iron frying pan.

Her leg had stopped bleeding. She glanced at the wall. The vein, though it had quit throbbing, still stuck to the wall. A thin trail of scarlet meandered down the wall like the capillaries that weaved across her legs. But no matter. Spider veins, though unsightly, were painless.

Though weak, she massaged her wet, numb leg. Shades of red pooled on the floor. Again, she inhaled the mixture of metal and alcohol. Did she imagine the leg pain had disappeared or had one pain replaced another? No matter, she was done—and she was alive. Could she stand? The room swirled. She'd rest until she regained strength. She eyed the whiskey bottle. A finger width remained. She downed it and closed her eyes.

Zack appeared. Unlike her, he was big and burly. He had taken after his father. Father and son hunted, roaming the woods near the cabin for game and small animals. Even as young as three, Zack had accompanied his father. Lilah had been against a child his age hunting, but Jeremiah won their arguments. Her husband towered over her. No hope in hell for her to win against him. Not then. But later—later when rage swelled and no one could stop her. Or had she been waiting for an opportune moment, that space of time between mirage and reality?

But the reality had happened. She'd been thrashed around one too many times. A younger Zack had stood by and watched and learned, and once, she had noticed his face, how he grinned; a spectator relishing the spectacle of a hen tossed into a cockpit. He had enjoyed the debacle, of course, because he did nothing to stop it. His eyes had sparkled like bubbly champagne corked open on New Year's Eve. Even when blood poured from her nose and curdling sounds spewed from her mouth and her face swelled and eyes blackened, he did nothing.

Later, he savoured being his own type of monster—her own son, whom she had carried for nine too-long months and laboured through a harrowing delivery. At almost eleven pounds, she had given him a head start in life. She'd cared for the fetus, eaten properly, exercised, done everything a conscientious pregnant woman should do. And breastfeeding. Oh, the pain upon swollen breasts—her once perky attributes—and nipples sucked until they cracked and bled, fluids drained dry until her boobs dimpled and deflated and sagged to her lumpy belly.

Yes, she had nurtured Zack like a proper woman, had put his health before hers. Jeremiah had watched and suckled, too, enjoying her warm milk, thinking it would make him stronger than Zack would ever be, stealing from her, stealing from Zack. Both of them stealing from her. In the end, Zack had morphed into another Jeremiah. And she'd never ever have the nerve to tell her son that his father had stolen from him.

As it turned out, she'd had enough milk for both of them. But later, her body had suffered. She became shrunken and frail. Despite that, she held her head high and her back straight and her legs sturdy. In front of her husband and son, she playacted, pretending she was a silly little miss. And she couldn't have more young'uns. I'll surely die if I do. She couldn't spawn another Zack. She had seen his eyes at birth, too big for his britches. And later, he'd enjoyed the kill, enjoyed the skinning and butchering.

But in the interval, that time between reality and mirage, time had passed, and too many innocent creatures had been maimed and killed. She grew fruits and vegetables in the garden. And herbs on the windowsill. And corn. How she loved corn on the cob despite hairs that persisted in sticking between her teeth.

Jeremiah and Zach gorged on red meat and white flesh. And they grew and grew in size. But not stronger—flabby, their minds weak with alcohol and wanton desires. And while she grew stronger and stronger, she plotted. Until one day....

The deed was done! Both deeds.

Lilah had been amazed a five-foot-two, blue-eyed, fair-of-face-framed-by-cornstalk-yellow-haired woman had accomplished the feat she'd plotted for years. She'd been most upset at killing her son. How could a mother do such a thing? But how could a son do what he had done to his mother? Both of them: like father, like son. It should have been like mother, like daughter, but she'd had no daughter. Might have had Zack not been born—had a female birthed first. And might have tried again had Zack turned out differently, but she hadn't wanted to spawn another child with Jeremiah. What would a daughter be capable of? She shuddered. Like mother, like daughter.

Both acts had been gruesome. Despicable for a lady of her stature. Acts uglier than varicose veins, but all her actions had been necessary to lessen pain.

Oh, how she detested and abhorred pain.

Jeremiah's and Zack's faces floated before her. On pedestals similar to those fanciful photographs of newborn babies swathed in leaves or sprouting from centres of flowers or cocooned in flowerpots. Yes, both faces before her: decapitated and speared with spikes. Scarecrows, both of them. And they succeeded in keeping crows and deer and rabbits and numerous other critters out of her garden. Her garden, healthy and wholesome with tomatoes and carrots and potatoes— vegetables that nourished her body.

After their deaths, she owed it to herself to enjoy the rest of her days without scum to hold her back. And she'd bedded every single man in town. And oh, how they wooed her. Wanted to marry her, procreate, for one as beautiful as her would surely produce beautiful babies like those in the popular photographs.

But no, she'd not produce again. One childbirth was enough. And she'd not marry again either. She'd not be one of those women who married and divorced and married and divorced. Three, four marriages? No, not for her. Once was enough.

And as she drifted off, remembering the past—had it been that long ago?—she saw Jeremiah's and Zack's faces where she had last visited them. High upon pedestals, skewered by iron posts, long hair swaying in winds of heat and cold and rain and snow until the species they had once plundered came to cart them away. And then all that remained was two pedestals in the field of cornstalks, metal points reaching to Heaven but stuck in Hell.

EXTERMINATED

By DJ Tyrer

"Run! You've got to run! Run for your lives!" Ted shouted as he burst out of the alley onto the quiet side street next to a small cafe.

Chairs clattered to the ground, cups shattered as they were dropped and half-eaten sandwiches fell from the hands of startled customers. The dozen or so people who had been enjoying the summer sun abandoned the pavement cafe to flee, but whether because of his shouted warnings or the fact that he appeared to be a madman dripping with sewage, Ted neither knew nor cared. He was already running at full-pelt, wishing his yellow overalls weren't so awkward to move in.

Then, it came flying from the alleyway after him, and those customers who had been glancing back at Ted screamed in terror and picked up their pace.

***

Ted worked in pest control. He used to work for the local council as an exterminator, but had been laid off "due to cutbacks." Strangely, the councilors and council's executives had all received wage increases way above inflation despite the cutbacks, plus hefty bonuses for all the savings they had made by sacking so many staff. But, Ted hadn't been bitter. In fact, he was grateful: without council operatives to do the job cheaply or for free, it meant people had to hire their own pest controllers and Ted had been raking it in. If they hadn't already been awash with the stuff, he might have bought his former bosses a bottle of champagne as thanks.

Mostly, these days, it was foxes that people wanted rid of. The things seemed to be everywhere and were brazen as anything; mangy creatures that wouldn't have survived five minutes in the country strode about as if they owned the town, gobbling up all the fast food that was dropped by drunks and yobs. People were the problem, of course, he mused as he parked his van up. People trashed the natural world and concreted it over, and then complained when the creatures moved into their neighbourhood to feast on their waste. But, still, as long as the idiots paid him to get rid of the vermin and didn't ask too many questions about just how ethical his "ethical entrapment" actually was, life was good.

But, today's job was rats. There were far more rats than foxes, but because folk seldom saw them and they didn't strut about like little kings, people seldom gave them a thought. More often than not, he got called in when one of the little blighters had died behind the skirting or down a drain and was causing a stink. Half the time, a house could be infested with rats and its human inhabitants would remain blithely unaware until one died and began to give off a nasty pong. People really were stupid.

Although maybe not today's client. Mr. Johnson was refurbishing a shop unit that had been empty since the economy tanked, and had realised it had been turned into a home for rats. Most likely, the blighters were living the good life on the food waste dumped in the bins of the cafe next door and whatever fats and things they flushed down into the sewers. A nice dry shop to call home and a ton of food within scuttling distance meant it was probably a rat's idea of heaven.

It was his job to turn it into hell.

Mr. Johnson was supposed to be waiting for him in the back alley, but there was no sign of the man as he stepped out of the van into the rubbish-strewn alleyway that ran behind the parade of shops.

A man stepped out of the narrow alley that ran between the shop and the cafe to deposit a torn black bag next to an overflowing bin. He was clad in a greyish, stained outfit known as kitchen whites and leaving a trail of peelings.

"Excuse me," called Ted. "Have you seen Mr. Johnson around?" At the man's blank expression, he added, "He's refurbishing the unit next to the cafe."

"No," replied the man, turning and shuffling back down the narrow alley to the cafe's side entrance.

Ted made a note to think twice about getting something to eat or drink from that cafe. Having seen many in greater detail than any health inspector, there weren't many restaurants or cafes Ted was prepared to eat at. Not even the fancy ones he could actually afford to dine at were up to much: they put all the glitz and glamour out front where the punters could see it and didn't seem to care that the kitchen was a cesspool.

He went over to the back of the unit and tried the door, which was rather grandly marked "Goods Entrance,"' despite being regular door size. It wasn't locked. That meant his client must already be inside. He was probably busy deciding which neutral shade of off-white to paint the walls or something.

Ted pushed the door open and stepped into a backroom fitted with empty shelves long devoid of stock.

"Mr. Johnson?" he called. "Hello, Mr. Johnson, it's Ted, Ted Grundy, the exterminator. Hello, Mr. Johnson, you there?"

There was no reply.

He could have been annoyed, but Ted wasn't. He charged by the hour and if Mr. Johnson kept him waiting, well, he would just add the time to his bill. Still, after a couple of minutes, he decided being paid wasn't worth being bored and, having already read the morning paper before he set out, decided to take a look around. It wouldn't hurt to spy out the lay of the land before he got started, see just what he was up against.

There was a toilet, a kitchenette and a cramped office off the storeroom. Mr. Johnson was in none of them. Ted could hear rats skittering about somewhere behind the skirting or under the floor and, when he opened the toilet door and flicked on the light, there was a plop, then a damp, sleek rat's head poked up over the rim of the bowl to gaze at him a moment before it vanished. He went over and looked down into the bowl, but it was gone; clearly it had slithered round the u-bend to escape down into the sewers below. He made a mental note that if he needed to use the throne, he would hold it in till he got home. His one at home had a macerator unit which meant he wasn't going to have any unwanted visitors popping up to see him.

Ted went through into the shop itself. The steel shutters were pulled down tight, but the lights were already on. A briefcase and a half-full mug of tea sat on a counter that had seen better days. He heard a rat run across the floor, but didn't spot it. A couple of holes had been chewed in the walls and clearly served as entrances for the rodents.

Well, his client had definitely been here. Possibly he had felt peckish and popped next door for a bacon sarnie. Or, as the flat over the shop was apparently a separate, albeit equally-abandoned property, he was down in the cellar, as that was the only part of the shop Ted had yet to examine. Even if he wasn't, he might as well take a look, familiarise himself with it.

He thought he had seen a trapdoor in the rear room, so went to check. Yes, there it was in the corner. It was shut, so it seemed unlikely Mr. Johnson was down there, but there was no harm in taking a peek. He always carried a flashlight on his belt along with other commonly-used tools, so took it from its holster and flicked it on before hefting open the trapdoor.

"Phoo-wee!" he exclaimed at the pungent smell that was suddenly released from its confinement. There was a definite tang of rat to the air, as well as the ripe stink of human waste underlying it. If he had to guess, Ted would have said the rats had probably burrowed a tunnel between their cellar home and their sewer superhighway. It was time to don his safety suit in case things got messy.

Ted returned to his van and pulled out the yellow rubberised overalls. He took his utility belt off, then struggled into the suit and the black reinforced wellies. Then he re-attached his utility belt and put on his facemask, gloves and goggles before pulling up his hood. He picked up a long, heavy stick that had proved itself many times over as a useful means of pest control.

Ready, he strode back to the shop unit. Got up as he was, it was easy to feel a bit of a twit, but he liked to imagine himself as a sort of superhero in his distinctive garb, out to rid the world of a few more pests: The Exterminator, the nation's unsung hero.

He carefully picked his way down the wooden steps into the cellar. He was a fairly big man who enjoyed his food, when he was confident it was vermin free. The stairs were fairly rickety even before being abandoned to several years of damp, and he felt a twinge of fear with every creak underfoot. But they held together, and a few seconds later he was standing on the damp, earthy, rat-dropping-strewn floor of the cellar.

He shone the torch around. This cellar was the size of the storeroom plus the little rooms off it. Pipes ran along the ceiling that clearly led up to the toilet and kitchen sink above. There was an archway to his right that had to lead into a second cellar below the main shop space. As he panned his torch about, the eyes of rats reflected eerily back at him, watching, and the occasional dark shape scampered away from the questing beam.

Ted felt a shiver of nerves and a drop of sweat ran down the length of his spine. There was something primal in knowing there were dozens, maybe hundreds of rats out there, surrounding him. He had never heard of rats swarming someone – when they acted en masse it was to flee as a group rather than attack – but it was easy to imagine they might. Despite knowing he wasn't in any real danger, he gave his stick a couple of experimental swings just to reassure himself.

A rat scampered inquisitively towards his foot, so he took a swing at it, but it scuttled away at the beginning of the movement. That was why they didn't bother with clubs and dogs these days. Lay down some warfarin and your problem hemorrhaged away with the minimum of effort.

He went over to the arch of bricks. Yep, the smell of sewage was stronger here. He shone his torch through. Piles of brick and earth were strewn about and it was clear the walls separating cellar and sewer had given way and collapsed. He was surprised the road and half the shop weren't down here with him. There also appeared to be pits in the floor, hinting there was a sinkhole here that the cellar was falling into. Some seemed shallow and had pooled with sewage, but a couple seemed deep.

"Well," he muttered to himself, "it looks as if my job is over before it's even started."

He was going to have to call the council and they would have to come and seal the area off before it really did come tumbling down into here. His client wasn't going to be best pleased.

Then, he spotted Mr. Johnson and realised he wasn't in a position to care anymore. In fact, there wasn't much left of him.

Ted vomited. This proved an especially unpleasant experience for him as he was still wearing his facemask.

Carefully, he peeled the mask away and tossed it and its contents onto the floor, before wiping his face on his sleeve to get the rest of the remnants off. A rat scuttled over to perform a taste test and he swung his stick absently at it, but was too horrified to really care and it only retreated a foot or so before returning to try again. Without his facemask, the unpleasant odour of the place was even worse.

Johnson's body was over by one of the piles of bricks and Ted wondered if the wall had collapsed on him, killing him. Or, had the man had a heart attack when he saw just how bad the cellar was? The rats had moved in to eat his flesh – a few were still daintily stripping bone, unconcerned by the torch beam fixed on them. Then, it struck him: how long could Johnson have been dead for?

He had spoken to the man last night and he had said he was home. The tea upstairs had seemed tepid rather than cold. He had been certain Johnson had arrived to open the place up for him. He couldn't have been down here very long and yet the rats had already practically stripped most of the flesh from his bones.

Ted felt scared. He told himself the rats couldn't have been responsible for the man's death, although he couldn't quite convince himself. But, now they had tasted human flesh...He shivered.

Something moved near him and he shone the torch beam down at it. It was a ratking. Ted had heard of ratkings, but he had never seen one before. There were seven rats, large ones, their tails tangled together in a chaotic knot. He stared at them in surprise and was even more surprised that they stared back with such a steady and, he hardly dared think it, intelligent gaze. He had always imagined the rats caught up in a ratking amusingly and futilely pulling in every direction, tightening the knot, but those facing away from him had shuffled around to face him and all seven stared as one.

As he looked down at the ratking, Ted became aware that other rats were creeping out to take up positions upon the various mounds of rubble. He was, he realised, slowly being surrounded. It was ridiculous to think of the rodents plotting this as if they had minds, and yet... he turned and ran.

Suddenly, something struck his shoulder and he heard his suit tear. He stumbled and, losing his balance, tumbled with a splash into one of the sewage-filled pits. He bobbed in the noxious liquid, arms flailing for what felt like an eternity, until he realised his feet touched the bottom. His torch had spun off somewhere amongst the rubble, leaving only a faint glow to illuminate the cellar. The ratking sat on the edge of the pool, watching him, as if waiting for him to make his next move. It was quite unnerving and he began to feel as if he were up to his neck in it proverbially, as well as literally.

With difficulty, he pulled himself up out of the sewage-filled pit. He was dripping with stinking filth, but found he didn't really care. He had lost his stick when he fell; never had he wanted it more.

Again, with unexpected suddenness, something struck him. He felt claws gouge multiple lacerations across his cheek and shoulder. With a shock, he realised it had been the ratking that had struck him.

Ted span around: the ratking was sitting atop one of the mounds of tumbled earth and brick, staring at him.

Again, without warning, it came at him, although this time, he had the chance to duck aside and narrowly avoid it. He could hardly believe his eyes, but the seven rats comprising the ratking had managed to launch themselves simultaneously into the air, spinning as if they were a ninja's throwing star. It was ridiculous! It was bizarre! It was impossible! And, yet, he knew what he had just seen.

They – it? – leapt into the air again, spinning towards him, but already he was running or, at least, waddling as fast as he could in the heavy overalls.

Rats swarmed out from crevices and hiding places in pursuit of him. The ratking span past him, narrowly missing his head. Then, he was in the first cellar. The trapdoor had closed –

had it fallen shut itself or had the rats somehow contrived to close it? Right now, almost anything seemed possible as panic and fear grasped him. With the faint glow of his torch trapped on the far side of the arch, the first cellar was in almost pitch-blackness.

He could hear the rats massing in the darkness. He tried to remember: where were the stairs? He thought he recalled it. He was fairly certain there was nothing on the floor to trip him. He decided to run.

Moments later, his shins smashed into the steps. Pain flared, but he didn't care: the agony of the blow was like a pronouncement of sanctuary.

The ratking slammed into his back and, this time, he felt claws dig into his back as it held on. Without thinking, he flipped himself so that he crashed, back first, down into the stairs. They shattered beneath him, but the ratking let go.

Ted stood, unsteadily and painfully. He reached out: the staircase was there. Although the lower steps were smashed, the frame seemed sound. With difficulty, he pulled himself up onto the upper section of steps. Reaching up, he felt the trapdoor's rough surface and pushed up, opened it. He scrambled out. As he regained his footing, rats began to pour from the toilet and out into the backroom. He didn't pause, he just ran outside. From the corner of his eye, he thought he saw the ratking spin up from the cellar.

Out in the alley, his immediate thought was to run for his van, but he saw rats sitting inside the cab. He couldn't believe it, and yet...

He ran to the narrow alley between the empty shop and the cafe. Already, rats were tumbling out through the shop doorway after him.

Ted burst out from the alley and onto the street.

"Run! You've got to run! Run for your lives!" he shouted as he burst out of the alley onto the quiet side street next to a small cafe.

Chairs clattered to the ground, cups shattered as they were dropped and half-eaten sandwiches fell from the hands of startled customers. The dozen or so people who had been enjoying the summer sun abandoned the pavement cafe to flee, but whether because of his shouted warnings or the fact he appeared to be a madman dripping with sewage, Ted neither knew nor cared. He was already running at full-pelt, wishing his yellow overalls weren't so awkward to move in.

Then, the ratking came flying from the alleyway after him, and those customers who had been glancing back at Ted screamed in terror and picked up their pace.

It struck his shoulder and he fell to the pavement.

"Help me!" he called to the fleeing cafe customers, but although a few glanced back at him, none paused to help.

The ratking was crouched beside him and more rats poured from the alley mouth out onto the street. In a single motion, as if a single creature, the ratking leapt upon his back.

"Please, help me!" he screamed, but none came.

He remembered Johnson – what was left of Johnson – and knew what his fate would be. He was about to be exterminated.

He swore, then shrieked in agony as sharp teeth tore at his flesh and his blood poured out through his torn yellow suit to stain the paving slabs.

I PRAY

By Essel Pratt

Every day I pray. Every day I prey. That is why I pray.

I'm a horrible person, lowest of the low. Never, growing up, did I think life would turn out the way it has. Life was good, coddled by loving parents and all the necessities one might need to survive comfortably without need for want or wanting for needs. Lessons abounded within my little world, teaching right from wrong and wrong from right, never embellishing the truths with damning recourse. Life was good, yes it was.

So, why is it, that here I am in this state of habitual desolation, detached from reality and embedded into euphoric nirvana within my sturdy skull. Was there some tragic incident that marred my mind and misshaped my perception of this ever-in-flux reality? Has my inner despair converted existence into a pawn of unexpected behaviors? If only I knew, if only I cared.

I've become a master of illusion, a captain of calamity, a specialist in misdirection and deceit. I'm no magician, but I can make you disappear without a trace, erasing you from the world without a morsel of haphazard thought within my head. I cannot control myself; I am what I've become. No more. No less.

I've met you in the bars, at the park, in the store. We've exchanged pleasantries, chattered about the weather, discussed politics and war. Yet, you've no idea who I am, no inkling of what meanders through my mind. My desolate deviance determines the definition that I allow you to believe I am. I guess I'm a sucker for such mind games. If you only realized what I am inside, I'd lose you forever.

Every day I pray that we will become one, embraced in love's cocoon. I watch you from afar from the sun's retreat behind the horizon until the moon's surrender to the day's first shine. I know you better than all you've met; black coffee, lemon meringue, patchouli perfume, and that plain white T. Everything about your aura has entranced me into your world, drawing me ever so close to your heart. I pray to feel your warmth against my flesh, the saturation of your love suffocating me from the inside out. I pray that we will be together for the eternity that I know we should.

Until then, I continue to pray and watch and learn.

***

Sitting alone upon this contoured metal chair, shifting my numbing posterior to avoid the agony I so often endure, I hope for your company. Knowing resolution is not at hand. Your shimmering skin accentuated by noon's distinct illumination. Your blue eyes glisten and your pearlescent smile hypnotizes me from afar. I hide my stare, but never avert my gaze.

The way you grasp your warm coffee mug, siphoning the heat into your soul; I long to be held in that embrace. My heart beats hard and fast, pumping blood through my veins with damning life. I count to ten, readying myself to stand and walk past you, inhaling the sweet smell of your perfume. Hoping you will notice and ask me to join you. I do not stand, instead I remain seated, uncomfortable, un-relaxed. Oh why do you captivate me so?

I start the count again.

1...

2...

3...

An Adonis approaches you, blonde curly locks flowing freely under the rotating ceiling fan; you burst from your chair and wrap your arms around his neck, pecking his cheek with your moist red lips. My heart dives into the pit of my stomach and anger fills the gap that is left behind. You are the love of my life. You have betrayed my trust.

I remain seated, sipping my bitter brew, although it has become as cold as my soul. Ice fills the blood in my veins. My thoughts retreat behind enemy lines, giving control to the demons inside. I am replaced.

I watch as you and he laugh at jokes that are unfunny. I observe your hands rub one another, fingers touching, souls becoming one. Lumps congeal within my throat as I hold back vomitus reflexes. I'll be damned if I allow your defiance to determine our fate. I hate you right now, loathe who you have become, want nothing more than to storm to your side, lift you from your seat, and carry you away from the devilish man that has stolen your heart. It is my heart. It is my prize. It is my desire.

The world fades to black as I give in to myself. What comes next I do not know, nor do I care. I know how it will end; with you by my side.

***

I prey. There is no other way to define what I am and what I do. Darkness encompasses my being, I am no longer in control as instinct takes the wheel and guides me on a path of destructive devastation. I am damned. You are damned. I know not what I will do. Yet, I still remain seated, observing the situation from behind the fog in my mind. My heart still beats with intense frustration as I collect the hatred for that man alongside the rejection you have dished out. The worldly sounds around me blur together in a gelatinous blob of a symphonic hate march.

I wait; contemplating my next move, searching for answers, struggling to sort through the confusion that floods my mind. The pressure from within is nearly unbearable. My skin crawls with anticipation as I wait. My gaze focuses solely on your face. You glance my way a couple times, noticing my stare. I fumble with the sugar packets in front of me, adding the horribly sweet crystals to my black nectar. I take a sip, nearly gagging on the sweetened drink, almost feeling my teeth rot on contact. I need a cigarette and fresh air.

***

It seems like an eternity, but I finally rise to my feet, dropping three dollar bills onto the table, and meander outside to clear my head. There is no other path by her side. I walk slow, steady, with a destination in mind. Yet, as I pass by I inhale her perfume. I want to grab her tight and take her with me, but I do not. I continue walking, her scent still in my nostrils, her essence inside me.

As I approach the heavy glass doors, the posterior reflection provides a final glimpse of her beauty. I open the door and emerge out into the world, the midday air erasing her scent from my olfactory glands. A part of me feels like it dies inside, but I continue onward to smoke my cigarette, anticipating the relief it will provide.

The hustle and bustle within the corrupt street forces me to seek solace within the side alleyway. I am shaded by the towering red brick façade, hidden from the view of the passersby, tucked away with only my thoughts and demons. Cigarette pressed tightly between my lips, I raise the lighter to the tip, allowing the flame to linger two seconds too long, feeling the heat upon my nose. It is not enough pain to make me flinch, but just enough to remind me that I am alive, despite being dead inside.

I take a puff, enjoying the tickle of the warm fumes infiltrating my wind pipe and congregating inside my lungs. Holding the carcinogens in until the strain can be held no more, I release. Spectral exhalation captivates my gaze and I wonder if the demons have finally released their grip on my soul. They have not, it is just a farce. It is just an illusion. I wish I was a magician, able to make the pain disappear. I am not. I am a lie.

As I stand there, in the shadowed alley, I lose myself in thought. Yet, nothing that filters through my head makes sense. I repeatedly ask myself why. Why am I this way? Why did my childhood morph from innocence to dissonance? Simply why? I receive no answers. Why would I? I don't know myself, I don't understand myself. How can I answer?

As I stand, sucking down the putrid fumes, the familiar click clack of heels on concrete rips me from peaceful thought. She is near me, I smell her close by. Without warning, she is right beside me, her purse strap snapping as if fate has finally intertwined our destinies. My heart skips a beat and instinct takes control.

"Shit," she says.

The voice is that of a goddess, the word expelling more meaning than an entire dictionary of revelations. I drop my cigarette to the moist ground, distinguishing its flame underneath my size eleven rubber soles, and drop down beside her, offering unneeded assistance as I help gather her scattered belongings. She is beautiful, she is a goddess.

"Oh, thank you," she says, her blue eyes meeting my own. "But, I think I have this under control."

I don't speak, just return a smile as I grasp her wallet and place it in her hand. Our skin touches and electric impulses invade my every pore. I have no choice but to give in to desire. I have no choice but to let the hidden me take over as I slip my left hand into my jacket pocket, carefully opening the zipper locked plastic bag with my index finger and thumb, prudently removing the moist cloth from within.

A quick glance around, I notice the street has emptied, if only for a second, and take the opportunity to raise the cloth to her face, forcing the chloroform into her lungs, waiting for her to fall asleep in my arms. She does not struggle, she gives in, she becomes mine.

Today I prey.

She has given in to me and I accept her embrace. My arms propped under her arm-pits, I hurriedly drag her limp body to the rear of the alley, behind the duo of dumpsters that provide a curtain of protection from passersby. She is mine; I cannot let her get away.

Glancing around, to ensure there are no hidden windows into my back alley utopia, I notice only graffiti on the wall. It reads, "Obey." It is what I do as I prop her body against the wall and place a single kiss upon her lips. The softness sends shivers down my arms, coercing a gaggle of goose bumps upon my flesh. I need her by my side forever, so I do what I know.

I slip my hands behind her back, underneath her shirt, carefully removing her ivory lace bra. I am cautious not to slide it down her arms, not completely removing it from her body. Respectfully, I slide my left hand up her shirt, grasping her left breast between my fingers. Her supple bosom feeds my veins with erecting blood, but I ignore the urges that attempt to control me. I am not here for pleasure. I am here for eternity.

Worried she might wake, I hold the cloth to her face once again; another dose of sleep. Satisfied, I remove the yellow rubber dishwashing gloves from my other pocket, stretching them over my readied hands before grasping her left breast once again with my left hand. With the other, I hold a blade. With another kiss planted firmly on her succulent lips, I slice deep into the base of her breast, a hole wide enough to my fist, and drop the knife into her lap before reaching deep inside, cracking ribs, and grasping her still beating heart.

Her body quakes and I play tug of war with her organ until victory is mine and her heart is in my grasp outside of her vessel. Her eyes open upon death. I gaze deep within; I see that she loves me. I see that she accepts my proposal.

Discarding the chloroformed cloth, I place the heart in the same baggie, and prepare the body for its final rest. Wiping the blood away with a nearby wash towel, most likely left by an impatient maintenance man, I ensure she is left in peace, without harm. Satisfied, I replace the brazier where it was, clasping it against her still warm chest.

She is still beautiful, even in death, but now I have her life and her heart. I am pleased beyond comprehension as I remove the bloodied gloves and discard them into the dumpster closest to us and place the plastic bag into my pocket. I stand, light another cigarette, inhale the noxious fumes, and become one with life and death. The dizziness fades and the confusion disperses. I am me once again. I am whole.

As I walk toward the street, prize in hand, I realize that today I preyed; a successful hunt.

***

Standing on the sidewalk, the sunshine beating upon my face, I absorb the rays and happiness nudges its temptation into my pores. Rarely am I happy; today I am. Today I found love and love found me. So I walk, homebound is my destination, passing by the tiny coffee shop within where I met my love. I glance at her table, wondering if Adonis is still there, waiting for his desire to return. In his place is a tiny brunette. I've seen her before.

Speaking to a waitress, I observe her lips request a black coffee. My drink of choice. She is beautiful. I wonder what her name might be, but I do not venture inside and inquire. Rather, I linger for a few seconds, observing her, wondering if she will return tomorrow. I decide to head home, not to linger any longer for fear someone might take my heart from me, with the new woman's presence stuck in my mind.

I decide I will return to the coffee shop at this time tomorrow, glancing at my watch to see that it is 1:36 in the afternoon, a time I don't normally arrive. My own heart beats hard as the silenced heart in my pocket awaits its place upon my shelf at home. I'll return, but not before placing my present love on the pedestal she deserves. However, tomorrow I will return. I will observe. I will decide.

Tomorrow I will start anew.

Tomorrow I will begin the courtship.

Tonight, however, tonight I pray.

FULL MOON

By Lance Hyden

When it comes to roommates, John is the king, the champion, the master, the bee's knees. Okay, I'm getting a little carried away. I guess what I'm trying to say is that he's an awesome dude and my best friend. Living together in a studio apartment we should be best friends! In this place everyone's business is everyone's business. He takes a shit with the bathroom door wide open, so I have no shame in dropping bombs on Baghdad in front of him either. We enjoy the same television shows; Star Trek is our all-time favorite. We listen to the same music; we always enjoy a good Simon and Garfunkel melody. Surf the same internet sites on his laptop; can't go wrong with YouPorn and Redtube. John's got complete control over all of our viewing and listening pleasures, except when he's not home of course. I probably should mention that he pays all the bills, including rent.

John's the Vice President for a large toy company and makes serious bank. Our studio, which isn't cheap, is at the top floor of a newly built high rise with a great view of Downtown Phoenix. He moved me in here about a year ago and has no problem with me staying here expense free. John's got a heart the size of Texas or Alaska, whichever one's bigger. He often says he would rather live like this then bring in some annoying douche bag that will pay half the rent.

Oh, I almost forgot, speaking of douche bags. We have another roommate, and this living piece of shit, goes by the name of George. He's possibly the laziest creature on the planet. He puts sloths to shame. What kind of name is George anyway? Sounds like the name of that dork kid picked last in kickball during

4th grade gym class just edging out Skylar, the kid with two left feet. Anybody still named George in this day and age should get their ass kicked on a daily basis just for general purpose. I guess you can assume by now I truly despise his existence. Take the name John for example, it's strong and intelligent, and will last for all eternity. Even my name, Sammy, holds more water than George. It should be in the same class of names as Barry, Neil, and Adolf… endangered!

I often wonder what John sees in George, especially since he doesn't want to live with a douche bag. The only time I see that idiot move is for food or to go hangout at the park with John. Those are the moments I really get to enjoy the silence of our place and the absence of that beady-eyed fuck. Every time they return from the park, George immediately collapses like he just ran a marathon at a Kenyan's pace. The lazy fuck doesn't even wash up. John goes right to the shower and clearly looks more physically fit than that stinky bitch face.

John loves to cook. I don't eat that much so two meals a day is fine. I'm not a free loader like George, who shoves everything down his huge throat into his obese stomach like a living garbage disposal. I would love to work and help with the bills, but there's nothing that's a perfect fit. My first and most recent job had me running around catering to the customers just for their fucking amusement. John got me out of that gig and I'll always be thankful to him for that. George doesn't even know what the word work means. He's like one of those sacks of shit that could work if they want to, but would rather collect disability milking the system. He's to fucking lazy to do that, so he mooches off John instead. He's probably one more hamburger away from a motorized scooter. Thanks tree hugging liberals!

I keep my opinions about that fuck-face to myself; it's not my place to show my distaste for him in front of John. After all, he was living here before I arrived and he's known George his whole life. Hopefully, he'll do something so stupid and unforgivable that John will be forced to kick him out. Then it would just be my best friend and I living the bachelor life, like Tom Hanks and that other dude in Bosom Buddies.

John brought home an attractive woman awhile back and after a couple hours of drinking wine, watching TV, and making out they decided to remove all their clothes and get into John's bed. I pretended to be asleep and not stare at them like a creeper. George had other thoughts. He decided, since we're all so close and live in one room, that we should share everything. He jumped into bed with them and began licking the woman like a freak. John quickly yelled at George to get the fuck out of here. He quickly retreated back to the couch and just laid there moping, but still watching them like a fucking psycho. I couldn't help developing this satisfying grin that I stealthily hid from them. A few more dumb ass moves like that and he'll be gone, and presenting the John and Sammy show!

I've never had sex and I'm pretty sure George hasn't either. Who would have sex with that filthy beast? John's a great looking a guy and has no problem in the sex department. I just haven't met the right one yet and staying cooped up all day in this place doesn't help. I'm sure John will hook me up with some cutie before that fat fucker. He's probably waiting so it's just him and I, then he won't have to find some smelly lard ass bitch for George.

Several months ago John invited over some guy he met from one of the websites we frequent called Craigslist. I didn't like the guy at all, really fucking weird. Still better than George though. I'm almost positive I saw him take some money from John.

He showed John something we've never seen before. The man kept referring to it as "going to the suburbs." After he applied gel to some humming long black stick thingy, he proceeded to thrust the black rod toward John's butt. I thought, "Wow! Where did it go?" He then slowly pulled it back out and I realized exactly where it went...his asshole! He repeated this numerous times and, even after watching all those websites with John, I didn't know that was an option. John seemed to be in pain at first but eventually started enjoying it. This was the coolest fucking thing I'd ever seen. He was introduced to a whole new world and John quickly became a frequent flyer. Ever since that day John's been "going to the suburbs" at least three times a week. His choice of items to take to the suburbs is different all the time. I haven't seen that creepy dude since that day, but I don't think John was attached to him anyway.

John never talks to us about it and goes through with it as if we aren't even here. I think he believes we're asleep or distracted by the television. George just stares at him with that dumbass mindless look he usually wears, while I try not to watch. I often have to glance over to see what new items he'll shove up his anus next. He really enjoys it and as a virgin I have to wonder if there's something truly amazing about this. Most of the time he does it alone, but occasionally he'll bring another man or men home to share the experience. Although, I have noticed that he never does this with women. I'm assuming they probably don't find it very pleasurable since they have a different hole to stick things in.

Three months ago John had this younger guy, again from Craigslist, over and he seemed better than that weird dude. We ate dinner and watched some TV for a while. I fell asleep and was awakened by sound of moaning. When I looked over at John's bed the young guy was on all fours with the bathroom plunger sticking out of his ass. John moved it right and left numerous times with his right hand and stroked the guy's dick with the left. About an hour later the young man left and said "thank you for spelunking with me." I guess there are different names for this type of activity. I'm curious why John's never included me in "spelunking" or "going to the suburbs." Not involving George I can get, but why not me? I'm sure it's just a matter of time, we're tight like that.

A few weeks ago we had a big scare. John was making a sandwich and he got the urge to go "coal mining" with a pickle…Dill. He looked troubled after a couple of minutes. When he came around from the kitchen island I noticed that the pickle was no longer in sight. At first, I thought it probably fell on to the floor or he threw it away without me noticing. After I realized he was walking funny and in a panic, I knew at that moment the pickle was sucked into his black hole. He didn't look to me or George for assistance; I choose to ignore what was happening so I wouldn't embarrass John. I wanted to help but George was clueless as usual and laid there asleep slobbering all over himself. What a tremendous stupid fuck wad!

John quickly reacted and pulled out a fork from the silverware drawer. I thought "brilliant thinking John, he'll use the fork to retrieve the pickle." After about fifteen minutes of pushing, pulling, wiggling and yanking on the fork, the vinegar and brine preserved cucumber, now deeper in his ass, was joined by a stainless steel dinner fork barely visible to the naked eye. The only option John had at this point was to call an ambulance. There was nothing I could do to help, I felt like George for the first time, fucking useless.

After avoiding every detail he could to the 911 operator, the paramedics finally arrived at 8:12 p.m. That was the longest eleven minutes of my life. It felt more like 8 hours. After closely observing John's backdoor and the situation he's in, they decided not to try and pull out the pickle but to radio back to the hospital. One of the Paramedics relayed a message to the hospital, "we have a zero dark thirty coming in."

You could hear slight laughter in the background during the return voice, "Should we prepare for a hunt for red October?" Now the paramedics are trying not to laugh. "That's correct; we have traffic in the Lincoln tunnel." The laughter on the receiving end of the radio is now bursting out loud. It appears that the medical field has their own terms, and not very professional, for removing objects from someone's stink hole. He was rushed off to the hospital with his parting words to George and me, "I'll be back soon boys."

John returned home about five hours later with the young man from three months ago. He had called him for a ride back from the hospital. I listened to John telling him that he underwent two procedures to remove the dill pickle and the four pronged eating utensil.

First was a rectal foreign body removal, the actual medical term, not the hunt for red October, zero dark thirty, or traffic in the Lincoln tunnel; insensitive pricks. Next, he had to get a Sigmoidoscopy, a procedure to look at areas of the colon and rectum for any issues caused by the foreign objects. Luckily, John suffered no damage to his shit dispenser and would only be sore for a few days.

After two weeks of lying low, light exercise, and cautiously wiping his ass after taking dumps, John was back to full strength and resuming regular activities, including shoe horning. Every week I learn a new term from John and his increasingly growing group of friends that engage in this act, almost like their own fight club, except it's more like stick things in my ass club. Sometimes they have ass play parties with anywhere from five to ten guys. They're like a secret society of anal illuminati. John must have told them that George and I aren't interested because they never bother us or try and get us to be a part of their corn holing. Sometimes it hurts my feelings that John never thinks I'd be interested. If he ever included George before me, I'd be devastated. The thought of that dried up cum stain being included in one of John's activities makes me furious, or jealous I suppose. I know John would never do that to me and it's just a matter of time before I'm a part of the action.

Tonight's going to be another full moon night, because John's young friend is here. John pulls out his box of ass toys from under his bed. It's full of different ass probing items, lotions, and lubricants. The young man lubes up his asshole with K-Y jelly in preparation for what is about to come. John pulls out an item I have yet to see; a clear plastic tube about 2 foot long and a 3 inch diameter. When did he get that?

John carefully inserts it into the young man's ass. That's got to hurt, but he seems to enjoy it. About 1 ½ feet still remains sticking out of his bunghole, but it's firmly in place. The tube's diameter spreads the young man's asshole wide open like a Florida sinkhole. John then grabs something out of the refrigerator and drops it into the small tube. I can't make out the item as it quickly slides down the tube and straight into the young man's dark portal.

John begins walking over towards me. Shit! Do I pretend to be asleep or busy? I close my eyes and lay there facing the opposite direction. I feel John's hand grab me. A rush of excitement rushes throughout my body. He's lifting out of my glass box and we're heading over to the young man and the plastic hollow dick sticking out of his underpass.

I look down to see George laying on the carpet looking up at me. I quickly drop four little pellets of shit on George's head to clear out my poop shoot in preparation. Ha! John's picked me to participate and not that stinky, ball licking, big nosed, four legged, ass eater George. Hey George! You can always try and stick your tail up your ass, you son of a bitch. This is the best day ever. Thank you John, I love you!

I can't wait to see what my part is. I hope he starts me off with something small and easy to put in my ass, like a pen or AAA battery... Duracell please! I'm so nervous but anxious too. I just wish John would have fed me before this, I'm fucking starving. Or perhaps it's a better experience on an empty stomach. So much to learn!

John lifts me up and looks into my eyes. "Have fun Sammy, just make sure you comeback out." Wait, what? Comeback out? What the fuck is he talking about?

He places me into the clear tube and I begin to slide down the shaft unable to stop myself. I smack right into the young man's asshole almost falling straight in. I cling to the fleshy sides, gripping to an ass zit, trying not to be swallowed up into this dark abyss and become a zero dark thirty or a finding Nemo.

I can hear John talking into the tube. "Go ahead little buddy, get in there." I don't really want to. This isn't what I had in mind to be included into the Poop Troop.

The smell of cheese is overwhelming the ass stench... Mmmm, cheddar! I'm so hungry my stomach is growling and I now realize what came out of the fridge and into his crawl space. I understand why John didn't feed me tonight. He knows I can't resist cheese, it's my favorite. Damn it looks like a bottomless pit down there. Fuck it! I take a deep breath and boldly go where no gerbil has gone before, at least I don't think, and I sing to myself..."Hello darkness my old friend."

The rear end.

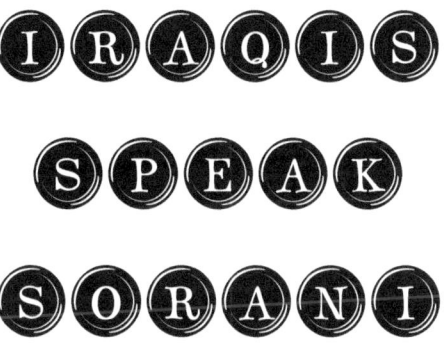

IRAQIS SPEAK SORANI

By Paul Rhodes

My blood looked black as it filled the syringe. I asked Nurse May whether she thought so too, but she didn't answer. Maybe the battery in her hearing aid needed replacing.

"Relax your arm," said Nurse May, sliding the needle from my vein with one hand, pressing a cotton bud onto the puncture with the other.

She sighed and shook her head, running her thumb up and down the bottle of blood, ironing out a kink in the label. WEEKES – Tobias, the label read, followed by my date of birth and outpatient number.

Something told me the decrepit Nurse May would outlive me. Back when I was a kid and I started having renal trouble, she looked old, but now with my failing kidney and toxic blood, she seemed damn near immortal.

Nurse May told me to go sit in the waiting room that my results would be along shortly.

It hurt to stand. My kidney was pounding again, and sharp twinges of gout stabbed at my ankles and knees.

Shuffling into the waiting room, I filled a paper cone of water from the cooler and gulped down an assortment of Colchicine, Tramadol and Co-codamol tablets.

The painkillers constipate me; Colchicine does the opposite. It's a coin toss, guessing what my wretched stomach will do next.

Christie, the clinic's receptionist, looked up from her text book to shoot me a critical glare as my shaking hands struggled to pop more pills from their blister packs.

Christie doesn't approve of my lifestyle, and likes to lecture me on the benefits of clean living. Coming to urology every Thursday, getting my arm jabbed, waiting for the day my kidney finally gives up - pissing Christie off makes it all bearable.

"Dr. Kierney insists I make you his last appointment of the day, you know that right?" Christie told me once. "So when you turn up drunk, you don't scare the other patients. Doesn't that embarrass you?"

Christie works out. I don't mean she exercises; I mean Christie works the fuck out. When she lifts that thick red hair to re-tie her pony tail, the muscles in her shoulders bunch in the middle. Watching her from across the waiting room each week, waiting for my results, I can't decide if her shoulders are getting bigger or her neck is getting shorter.

"All finished, Roy?" Christie beamed at the monstrous yellow cyst riding a mobility scooter silently from the corridor that leads to the dialysis machines. Fat, jaundiced Roy; poured into a t-shirt and shorts. Jagged toenails poked out from broken leather sandals - Roy lives alone and can't reach his feet.

For someone that just had his blood cleaned, Roy didn't look too good.

End-stage kidney patients like Roy stink of piss. That's their body secreting urine through their pores when they can't pee it out fast enough. A cleaner with splotchy blue tattoos on her forearms wipes the clinic down twice daily to stop us all making it smell like a public toilet.

The stench of bleach mixed with the August heat seeping in from outside brought the heady sensation of falling. My shirt began to shrink wrap me where I sat, dark wet patches appearing wherever my skin touched.

Christie paused her conversation with end-stage Roy to glance over at me, rolling her piercing viper eyes, shaking her head with exaggerated turns.

I sat back in the chair, rested my head against the wall, and closed my eyes. It took me a minute to realise the hypnotic whir I was listening to was the low drone of the dialysis machines calling me from down the corridor.

Dialysis is living death. A last resort for when all the transplants in the world won't save you. I didn't want to end up there, lost in the maze of curtain sided cubicles, each with its own renal casualty. Yellow, soft-bodied creatures wired up to computers like science experiments; all that suffering just to exist.

I sat on my hands so Christie couldn't see how bad I was shaking. Blinking through sweat-stung eyes at burning visions of my fate – hooked up to a machine, withered and yellow, curled up in bed next to fat fucking Roy.

I was starting to unravel. Frantic, scanning the room for something to distract my rabid mind, I noticed the tattered posters, funded on a shoestring by the NHS.

Love your kidneys – stop smoking today – before it is too late.

Foreboding of death, they hung from the wall like a man left alone at the gallows.

Kinsure - lifelong security for you and your family – after you've gone.

Everywhere I looked was death and horror. Each poster bearing the same stock photo, some lost looking old bastard, peering back forlorn, ready for a bolt through the head.

Is hyperuricemia damaging your kidneys?

Only the corporations promised a life, their advertisements glossy and rich. A gleaming white cruise liner sailed on crystal waters under blue skies and a burning sun.

Can't take a holiday because of your dialysis commitment? Try Rena-Cruise - international luxury cruises for people with chronic kidney disease. A dialysis machine in every cabin!

Can you imagine a worse place for dialysis patients than on a boat in the middle of the ocean? Bent over with stomach cramps, sick from toxic blood. Bobbing up and down and side to side...all together now...bleeeeeuuuuuuuurrrrrrrggggghhhhhhh!

A life worth living if you can afford it – phone now for a free quote, all major credit cards accepted.

Fuck you Rena-Cruise and all you chicken-hawk companies trying to sell us a li(f)e. Fuck you, Christie with your red hair and big tits. And fuck you, Roy, and your big fat death sentence.

I clocked Christie and Roy watching me, and realised I'd been speaking out loud. Fatboy Roy even adjusted the controls on his chair, swiveling it around to face me with the kind of whoosh that elevator doors make.

Stumbling to my feet, knocking my chair back against the wall, the burn of my swollen ankles sent me flying across the waiting room. I blurted something at Christie, something about sending me the results of my blood test.

"You think you're so much more deserving than everyone else, don't you?" Christie snapped, as I lurched toward the exit. "Showing up drunk every week, knowing you'll get a kidney when you need one. What about people like Roy? He's been on dialysis for years because of his blood type."

"Roy may not drink but he sure as hell eats enough," I shouted back, "or hadn't you noticed that, Christie? You gonna preach to Roy about his fucking calorie intake?"

Roy's eyes bulged and he started choking wildly, thrashing back and forth on his scooter. Christie leapt over her desk and began thumping Roy across the back with one of her pumped up forearms. From a distance, it looked like she was trying to kill him.

Staggering out the exit into the grounds of Medway Hospital, I looked back to see Christie, face as red as her hair, telling poor terminal Roy, calm down please, deep breaths.

**

Summer in Gillingham is dust that blows from nowhere. Broken glass and dog shit on the pavement, the smell of creosote on fences. Life in Gillingham is wandering without destination, beer in tall cans and painkillers in blister packs.

Dr. Kierney prescribed Colchicine after my kidney function took another nosedive and the Allopurinol I was using to filter uric acid from my blood began to poison me. The buildup of uric acid triggers outbreaks of gout. During a gout attack, I can't walk. Think somebody taking a soldering iron to your ankles and knees. The outside packaging of the Colchicine read, TAKE AS DIRECTED – STOP USE IMMEDIATELY IF SIDE EFFECTS OCCUR.

I didn't need to read the instructions to find out that too much of it gives me the shits. I could deal with that, I spent more time on the crapper but at least I could walk.

**

The last sticky heat of the day clung to my head and I watched, detached, as my body limped out into the middle of Canterbury Street and several sets of screeching tires.

"Get out of the fucking road, junkie!" a voice yelled from somewhere.

I didn't take offence at being mistaken for a smackhead. In Gillingham, people are either fat, cola-sucking benefit slobs, or skin-and-bone junkies. There is no in-between.

I tried to step out of the road but couldn't move. A sudden howling cramp in my stomach folded me at the waist. The lower half of my body shut down, and I flopped lifeless onto the boiling hood of a car that had skidded to a halt before me.

The door on the driver's side flung open and two thick, sweaty hands grabbed hold of my collar and belt, dragging me across the street to the pavement. A line of cars began to form, people yelling, sounding their horns, filming us with their phones. Four hard kicks drove into my stomach, a fifth landed across my face, snapping my neck back, busting my lip and nose.

Then the sweaty hands were gone and the traffic quickly disintegrated into the late afternoon haze, leaving only the taste of blood.

After a while, I propped myself up. Leaning back against somebody's garden wall I realized I was done with being sober. Four days in the bank and I hadn't seen the light, I didn't feel better, I just felt miserable and alone.

My stomach knotted again and I choked out a couple dry heaves. I tried swallowing some Tramadol pills but my mouth was sticky and they wouldn't go down. Crunching them up, the bitter powder coated my tongue, making me gag.

Is this rock bottom? If it's not, how will I know when I get there?

My default mechanism for moments like this is to trawl through my imagination's extensive rolodex of naked Christie scenarios.

This time she's on top of me, grinding my pelvis into salt, screaming, "You! Must! Stop! Drinking!"

Choking me, holding me down...

"You! Must! Stop! Drinking!"

And I'm crying, forcing my face into the bed sheets. Please Christie, no more! I'll do whatever you want!

Christie, my lord and savior, hurting me, telling me to trust her, it'll be OK. Christie, breast-feeding me like a child. A 30-year-old, fucked up child, sucking on those perfect tits. Christie, bathed in white light, guiding me back to the womb.

After a few minutes of Christie, I was able to stand. I set off down the street again, heading toward the BestSave mini mart. The blazing sun hung low in the sky and I stared into it until my vision doubled and a black dot appeared.

My phone buzzed as a text came through - Christie; Congratulations Mr. Weekes, your Filtration Rate remains at 20; you better go get drunk to celebrate.

Hands still shaking, it took several attempts to type my response – Thanks for letting me know, Christie. C U Next Thursday.

***

The queue inside the BestSave stretched back to the refrigerators. People grunting, shaking their heads, checking their watches like they had to be somewhere.

Nobody in Gillingham has to be anywhere. That's why they're in Gillingham.

The problem was with the clerks. The two Iraqi guys behind the counter were having trouble with the till.

Heading down the queue to the rear of the shop, I found the booze fridges and set my forehead on the cool glass. My bastard kidney wasn't giving up, pounding away at my insides, like that one neighbourhood kid who would spend entire Saturdays kicking his football against a wall rather than go home.

The brown red smudge my face made on the glass of the fridge looked like one of those gauze masks they put on burns victims.

I needed a hit of sweetness, something to wash away the blood and dust, soothe my body, and quiet my mind. I took two four-packs of Strongbow cider from the fridge, letting the glass door swing shut, and eyed the queue. Ten people, with full baskets of groceries; cursing under their breath, looking around at each other for recognition, in that very British way.

I'm going to moan about it but I'm not going to say anything until someone else does.

I stood one four-pack of tall cans on the floor, cradling the other like a newborn; the cold of the tins chilled the skin beneath my damp shirt. I needed to drink but that queue was not moving.

Everything was heightened; the garish colours of the cereal packets, the offensive symmetry of the rows of tinned food and ready-made pasta sauce, the unbearable scream of the light bulbs, the sniffing and throat-clearing of the customers in the queue, the dryness in my mouth, the cracks on my lips opening up into chasms. I was a nomad lost in barren land and I needed...

"Excuse me, are you in the queue?" an old lady asked. It was August, but she'd wrapped herself in a beige raincoat and tied her head with a pink and purple cotton scarf.

"Christ," she muttered when I didn't answer. "Doesn't anyone speak English in this bloody town?"

The Iraqis had the cash register in pieces now, staring blankly at each other, the receipt roll cascading onto the floor. These guys were not the store's regular employees.

I'm just going to step out for an hour, their boss told them. It's always quiet around this time. You'll be fine.

One of them dialed a number into a mobile phone, surveying his customers with unease. He was losing sympathy with the locals and he knew it.

"Fuck's sake, c'mon mate!" someone shouted, followed by jeers and taunts from the rest of the queue.

The younger of the two Iraqis looked at his friend, said something, and then hit redial. Whoever he was phoning was not picking up. The other Iraqi, broad shoulders and black beard, held up parts of the till to show the mob, offering an apologetic, gritted teeth smile.

I tore off a can of Strongbow and cracked it open. I'd explain when I got to the counter, they seemed like nice guys, they'd probably apologise to me for making me wait. Setting the remaining three ciders down, I put the cool tin to my lips and drained it in one go.

It didn't taste right. The cider had an artificial, synthetic flavour, metallic almost. Not the zinc taste of blood, the first couple swallows got rid of that. This was different.

I pulled open a second can and took a few gulps; there it was again, that awkward metallic taste.

Thinking it must be a dud batch, I opened a can from the other four-pack and took a slurp; same thing. I tried one more can of Strongbow from the second four-pack of tall cans but it was no different, that wretched chemical zing.

For some reason it reminded me of the bleach smell in the urology clinic.

Perhaps the Iraqis are selling counterfeit booze? The Lithuanians do it with vodka. The 57% shit they sell from under the counter. Alcohol best served as cleaning fluid or anti-freeze.

Something clicked inside my head as the awful reality of the scene hit me full force.

I'd rumbled a terrorist cell – the Iraqis had poisoned the Strongbow.

I walked back to the fridge, yanked the door open, tore open a can of Stella and gulped it down. Holy shit, they'd done the beer too!

It was genius; there are BestSaves all over the country. Why blow up a train when you can poison a nation, the drunkest nation on earth?

I tried the Heineken and the Budweiser; same toxic metallic taste.

I was wild now, swinging open the refrigerator doors, grabbing tins, tearing them open, gulping down mouthfuls of beer and cider and throwing them to the floor - Kronenberg, Coors, Amstel, Oranjebaum, Fosters...all contaminated.

An ISIS cell in Gillingham right under our noses; this was revenge for Saddam.

"Excuse me, Sir, what on earth are you doing?"

I turned to find the queue gone, and the younger Iraqi walking toward me. A wiry lad with dark murderous features, probably highly trained in the art of hand-to-hand combat from months spent in a training camp in Mosul.

"You cannot come in here and do this, Sir, you must pay now or I am phoning the Police."

I looked around at the half empty cans of beer and cider strewn across the floor. I was no match for him, not with my rotten kidney and arthritic joints.

"Phone the Police!" I shouted, hoping somebody passing by outside would hear and intervene. "And while you're at it, tell them to get the anti-terrorism unit down here, I think they'll be very interested..."

"Terrorist? You calling me terrorist, bastard?"

He threw a hard punch toward my face but lost his footing in the pool of beer and cider and slid onto the floor, bringing down several shelves of dried food from the narrow aisle with him.

I clambered over him and ran for the exit, only to find the big bearded Iraqi wedged in the doorway.

"You go nowhere until you pay!" he shouted, catching me around the waist and tackling me to the floor. We hit the ground hard with him on top, his shoulder plunging deep into my stomach.

An awful sound followed. Like someone throwing a bucket of water on to a patio.

The Colchicine had got me again - the seat of my pants, hot and wet.

The Iraqi realised what had happened before I did. His eyes bulging as we clinched, frozen in time, faces inches apart.

I was there – rock bottom.

I began to cry. Big deep sobs, and I wrapped my arms around his neck, burying my face into his chest, his thick black beard rough against my skin.

"I'm sorry Dad, I'm so sorry...I fucked everything up..."

Very slowly, I felt his arms spread out around me and the big bearded Iraqi gave my shoulder a gentle squeeze.

His colleague appeared from the aisle, ranting wildly, waving his arms. The guy on top of me turned to him and spoke quietly, in whatever language Iraqis speak. Raising himself away from my broken body, he offered me his hand, his face haunted and confused.

"You go now, Sir," he said. "Quickly, no Police, you just go."

And I shit myself again.

***

I was losing it, I felt sure of that.

Later that evening, all cleaned up and settled by beer and Co-codamol, I searched on-line to find out what language Iraqis speak. I'd go back there tomorrow and thank them; they'd be impressed if I apologised in their mother tongue.

I also read through the information that had accompanied my prescription.

The excessive use of Colchicine can produce many side effects, some more rare than others; everything from flu-like symptoms to multiple organ failure. Overdosing on the medicine may result in confusion, paranoia and hallucination.

The most common side-effects are nausea and diarrhea.

A small percentage of users reported a strange metallic taste.

BUMPS

By Phil Richardson

After Pam finished mowing the yard, she pushed the mower into one of the rickety sheds, and walked down the graveled path to their log cabin. She heard a scrabbling noise and looked up to see a woodpecker pecking at the roof which already needed fixing. She had told her husband Bryan to repair the roof a month ago, but he said he was afraid of heights. Bryan was always ready with an excuse not to do something but she loved him just the same. One of these days he might even find a job.

She slammed the screen door, walked into the front room and began picking up the bones and scraps of fat that were the remains from last night's supper that Brian had left, along with his dirty plate, on the coffee table. He seldom ate in the kitchen, usually parking himself in front of the TV and watching Jerry Spencer or, his favorite, Swamp Monsters That Eat You.

All he wants to do is watch that stupid TV and go hunting. Manly things! I'm about fed up with him. If he didn't have his disability pension from the army, we'd starve to death. Lazy bastard. But, he sure does know how to make a woman feel good. He sure is a randy bastard and he makes going to bed a pleasure.

But Bryan wasn't here to yell at – he had gotten up early to go hunting, and she, of course, had to get up early to fix his breakfast before he left. He mainly hunted alone because his buddies all worked at real jobs.

"See you about six," he had said as he shuffled out the door. "Have supper ready. I'll be hungry. Make sure there's cold beer in the fridge."

"Stay safe, Bryan," she said.

Pam bustled around the house all day picking up Bryan's clothes and the empty beer bottles, which he had tossed on the floor by the couch. Their cabin was smallish, so cleaning didn't take too long. That was a blessing because Bryan would walk in the door yelling "food" and "beer" when he came home. She never knew what time he would arrive, so she had to plan his evening meal to include something she could keep warm in the oven.

She finished her chores just before seven o'clock and wondered why Bryan was so late. It would soon be dark and even an experienced hunter could get lost after dark. She fussed and fretted around the kitchen and finally went outside and called his name. The shadows had lengthened and the woods around their cabin seemed closer than they did in daylight. She shivered, thinking of Bryan lost in the darkness of the woods. About eight o'clock, she shut off the oven, put the food in the fridge and went to bed.

She couldn't sleep that night as she kept expecting to hear the front door slam open and Bryan to call for his supper. By morning she was really worried. She hiked off into the woods calling his name but after a couple of hours of searching, she gave up.

By nightfall she was concerned enough to call Tom Blackburn, the county sheriff, who said he'd check all the usual places (meaning bars) that Bryan liked to visit. If he couldn't find him there, then he would organize a search party in the morning.

"Bryan will show up," he said. "He knows these woods and he isn't the type to shoot himself in the foot or anything. I've hunted with him a lot of times and he's got woods' savvy."

But Bryan didn't show up that day or the next.

When he had been lost in the woods for four days, Pam was beside herself. She paced up and down the living room of their small cabin and, once more, called the sheriff.

"Why can't you find him, Tom?" she sobbed into the phone. "It's been four days and you haven't found him."

"Pam, we're doing everything we can. We've got helicopters and dogs and trackers and there's not a trace of him. Besides, we've got other problems this week."

"What other problems could be as important as my missing husband?" Her voice was strident now.

"Well, people are claiming they saw flying saucers. Good people. Not crazies. We got to follow up on that."

"Are you out of your mind!" This time it was a scream and the sheriff could not calm her down. Finally, Pam hung up the phone – actually, she threw it across the room.

Just then the front door crashed open and Bryan stumbled into the room. He was buck-naked.

"Bryan!" Pam rushed across the room and hugged him. She jumped back and said, "Where are your clothes? Where have you been?"

"I…I…don't know."

"What do you mean?"

"I mean, I've been lost, I guess."

Pam pushed him away. "Where are your clothes? How did you get here? We've had people searching the woods. How come they didn't find you?"

"I think I was too far away. That's it. I think I was taken someplace far away…."

"Are you friggin crazy? Are you trying to tell me you were kidnapped by aliens?"

"I don't really remember. You know I wouldn't lie to you. I love you too much. You're gonna be the mother of my kids and we're gonna live together forever."

Pam smiled. She loved to hear him say that. Of course they had only been married for two years and forever was a long time.

"I'm calling the sheriff," she said. "He will come here and he will question you and you better be tellin' the truth."

The phone call took a while, because one of the reporters had come up with the idea that aliens had kidnapped Bryan, and that was a story with legs. The sheriff liked the publicity and he was playing it to the hilt.

"I'll be right over there, Pam," the sheriff said. "Don't dress Bryan up though. Cover him with a blanket and make sure he tells any reporters he was kidnapped by aliens."

"They'll think he's crazy. He can't say that."

"Just do it," the sheriff said and hung up.

Bryan sat on the couch, his head almost in his lap, and it was then that Pam noticed small bumps all over his skin--raised bumps the color of egg yolks.

"What happened to your skin?" Pam asked. "Did some nasty bugs bite you? I'll get some medicine or, better yet, I'll put some vinegar on it." Pam rushed to the kitchen for the vinegar and returned with some paper towels and the bottle. She poured the vinegar on the towel and started rubbing it on the bumps.

"Ow! Stop that, it hurts!" Bryan jumped up and pushed Pam away. Oddly, he was not scratching the bumps. Pam thought maybe the vinegar helped, but he wouldn't let her put any more on.

The bumps continued to grow however. After twenty minutes, they were about an inch wide and shaped like little pyramids. Pam wanted to touch them but restrained herself.

Bryan just sat there.

After about an hour, a loud thumping on the door announced the arrival of Tom the sheriff. Pam opened the door and he thundered into the room.

"Where the hell have you been, Bryan?" Tom asked.

"I don't know. I guess I was somewhere."

"You guess! We've had people and dogs and helicopters searching the woods. Didn't you hear anything?"

"I'm not sure I was in the woods."

"What's that on your face?"

"Bumps."

"If you weren't in the woods, how did you get bit?"

"I don't know."

Wham! The sheriff slammed his fist on the table. "Goddammit! I spent thousands of dollars lookin' for you and you don't know where you were?"

"Nope."

"Stop it, Tom!" Pam shouted. "You got no right to yell at Bryan like that. He is the one who got lost. You didn't find him. He found himself."

Tom stepped back as if afraid that Pam was going to hit him.

"I'm just trying to find out what happened," the sheriff said. "And, what are those bumps all over him?"

"Skeeters, maybe," Pam replied. "I put some vinegar on them. They're sure funny lookin' though."

Bryan lifted his hand to his face and pushed at one of the bumps.

"Almost feels like there's something alive in there," he said. "Like a worm or something."

"I never heard of a worm bump," the sheriff said. "Maybe you should get to the doctor."

"Look around you, Tom," Bryan said. "Does it look like we could afford to go to a doctor?"

"Maybe I could put some more vinegar on it," Pam said. "It'll hurt, but maybe that's a good sign."

"I want you in my office tomorrow morning," the sheriff said. "We got to get to the bottom of this. Can't have people wandering out in the woods and not being found and then showing up and not knowing where they was. Besides, I want you to talk to them reporters." He jammed his hat on this head and left.

Pam left the room to get the vinegar and Bryan stayed on the couch with the blanket wrapped around him.

"Pam! Pam! Come here quick."

Pam rushed back to see Bryan threshing around on the floor. He was slapping at his face and his legs and screaming in pain.

Pam looked on in horror as the bumps on Bryan's skin expanded and burst. She screamed and screamed because from each bump a small form splashed onto the floor.

Bryan rolled onto his stomach and the bumps on his back burst and more little figures fell onto the carpet.

"Oh My God!" Pam yelled. "Oh My God!"

Bryan shivered a bit and then was still.

The little figures twitched and turned and then stood on their two little feet.

Each figure was an exact replica of Bryan with a full head of hair and a mature-looking body. There were about fifteen of them but they were moving around so it was hard for Pam to count them. She was also in a bit of a shock.

"Bryan! Are you okay? Bryan what happened?"

Bryan was not okay. He did not answer and he was not breathing.

Pam didn't know what to do. The little bryans were yelling at her in high little voices, "Food! Food! Food!" So she took a broom and herded them into the other room. Then she called for an ambulance.

Even through the closed door of the other room, she could hear the little bryans clamoring for food, so she turned on the TV to drown out the sound. She didn't want anyone to know her secret.

The EMTs arrived about fifteen minutes later and, after working on Bryan for about twenty minutes, pronounced him dead.

Pam fainted.

They revived her and proceeded to haul off Bryan's body. One of the EMTs tried to talk Pam into going in for a checkup, but she refused. She knew she couldn't leave those little bryans alone.

After the EMTs left, the screaming from the other room got louder and Pam went to the kitchen and fried a bunch of eggs. She carefully opened the door to the room where the bryans were bunched up waiting for their supper. She placed the plate of eggs on the floor and stepped back as the crowd of bryans assailed the plate.

They weren't very polite.

They shoved and pushed and stuffed eggs into their mouths. Something almost akin to growling issued from their throats.

"Stop that!" Pam yelled. "Behave yourselves."

They paid her no heed and finished off the eggs, gathered in a circle and looked up at her.

"What do you want?" she asked.

"More food! Lots of food. Beer," they chorused.

Pam spent the next hour trying to fill them up and finally they all trooped over to the cat's bed and curled up to sleep.

Pam wondered about the cat. The bryans weren't much bigger than a mouse and would make a tasty bite for the kitty. She closed the door to the room and went looking for the cat. When she found her, she put her outside and breathed a sigh of relief.

What am I going to do? Bryan's gone, but I've got fifteen little bryans who I can't tell anyone about and I'm a widow and I don't know what is happening. Where did Bryan go in the woods? What did he do to bring all this upon us?

She decided to deal with it in the morning and went to bed. The cat was scratching at the door, but she didn't want to worry about the cat and the bryans so she left it outside.

The next morning she woke to the pleading voices of the bryans. "Water. Food. Help."

She fixed them a breakfast of cereal and milk and watched as they greedily devoured the whole bowl. As she observed them, she noticed they were getting bigger. Almost double the size of yesterday.

They sure grow fast. I'm gonna have to get some more food in. I wonder if they would eat cat food. They need clothes. I'll just make them some loincloths out of old handkerchiefs. They're growing so fast nothing else will fit them.

It turned out that they would eat cat food. They wouldn't however, use kitty litter and she began to find messes all over the room.

Although they all looked like Bryan and had his table manners, their vocabulary seemed to be limited. "Food" and "Water" and "Beer" were the words they most frequently used. After a few days, they were about the size of kittens and she decided to let the cat in the house again.

Maybe Kitty will adopt them. I've heard of cats adopting chickens and ducks and even puppies.

The cat would not go near them, however. It took one look and headed for the basement.

A month later the bryans were as big as a five-year old child. They seemed to be hungry all the time. Pam was running out of money, so she bought dry dog food and begged scraps from the butcher.

"Food not good!" the bryans threatened. They stomped their little feet and crowded around her. "More food!"

In order to buy more food, Pam sold her mother's silverware and the watch that Bryan had given to her on her birthday.

By this time, both the cat and the dog had disappeared. Pam wasn't sure whether they had fled or been eaten. She feared the latter.

She made some progress with the bryans. They went out to the woods to do their business (most of the time). They ate with spoons and forks instead of with their fingers (most of the time).

However, they watched TV all day (again, Jerry Spencer) and they never helped clean up the mess they left in the front room.

***

"More food!" the bryans, who after two months were almost four feet tall, filled the kitchen and shouted their mantra.

Pam got out the sack of Pedigree (with cheese) and filled several bowls. It was kind of funny seeing them at the table eating dry dog food with their spoons and drinking beer from a bottle to wash it down.

In addition to feeding them, she had faced the problem of clothes for fifteen bryans. She went to Goodwill and found enough clothes to fit them all and they reluctantly put them on. Although they looked more civilized, they still had bad bathroom habits so she forced them to spend more time outdoors.

Soon, she began to find the skeletons of birds and small animals scattered in the yard. The woods were strangely quiet as though most of the animals and birds had left—or been eaten.

She finally had to sell Bryan's truck to get money for more food and beer. She still had their old Ford sedan so she could go into town to buy food and beer.

The bryans were now as big as she was. After a couple of bad experiences, she made them sleep in the barn and she locked her bedroom door at night.

Then, one of the bryans disappeared.

She looked all over the woods and hoped she wouldn't find bones and she didn't.

The next day another bryan disappeared.

The sheriff called two days later and asked if she had seen two teenage girls, Patty Kelly and Megan Jones.

"They've been missing for three days now," he said. "It's not like them to run away even if they are kind of boy crazy."

"No, I haven't seen them," Pam said, "but I'll call you if I do."

"Sure are a lot of strange things happening around here," the sheriff said. "You be careful."

"I will," she said as she hung up the phone.

Two bryans and two girls. It adds up.

She was so worried she sat down that night and drank beer with the bryans. If you can't beat 'em, then join 'em. They all got drunk. Very drunk. In her drunken haze, it was easy to imagine that Bryan himself was there wherever she turned.

And turn she did.

When she got up the next morning, her bedroom door was unlocked, and all the bryans were in the kitchen devouring what food was left. There was no beer left.

Pam felt a little woozy and found it hard to believe what she was seeing. "Stop that!" she shouted as she began shoving the bryans out the door and into the yard. They grumbled, but let her do it. She counted them and two more were gone.

I won't call the sheriff to see if any more girls are missing. It would be too suspicious. Maybe they'll all go away and solve my problem. Maybe they'll go back to where they came from – wherever that is.

She stood there in the doorway for a moment and then, absentmindedly scratched at some bumps that had appeared on her arm.

Little bumps that she now saw were all over her body. Little bumps shaped like pyramids.

She wondered if they would look like her or look like Bryan.

PATTY HEARST HAS A GUN

By Sandi Sonnenfeld

Playboy, of course, is Erica's idea. It's Sunday afternoon, and Erica's parents have come to the Marks' house to play a round of pinochle.

Pinochle is Renie's parents' abiding passion. When they play, it's serious business. Out comes the special card table. Out comes the tray of cashews and dried Turkish apricots, which sits right next to the table, so that the players will have something to nosh on and Renie's mother won't have to get up in the middle of a hand to play hostess. Out come the scoring pads and pencils. And the bourbon and the vodka. Renie's parents only drink when they play cards, and even then Renie notices that her father uses his bourbon sour more as a prop than a beverage. Whenever he has a good hand, he will stop for a moment to take a long sip of his by now watered-down drink as though contemplating his strategy, and then immediately jump bids. Renie's father and mother then proceed systematically to decimate the opposing couple.

Renie's parents met Mr. and Mrs. Saunders at a pinochle party and really hit it off, Renie's mother said. They figure that if the grown-ups can become good friends so quickly, the two daughters can too, which is why over the past few months the girls have been thrown together for a series of "play dates." The fact that Renie thinks Erica is a bossy show-off doesn't seem of any concern to her mother.

Erica is thirteen, a year older than Renie, and captain of the JV cheerleading team. Tall, extremely thin, and perpetually tan, Erica is the first kid on her block to get a shag haircut just like Kristy McNicol's. The first girl at school to successfully blow a bubble within a bubble with her purple Hubba Bubba, and the first person in Seaview, Long Island (according to Erica, of course) to receive a signed picture of Tony DiFranco, the lead singer of the DiFranco Family.

"Isn't he the absolutely cutest thing in the world?" Erica said, the first time the two girls hung out together, and hugged the nine-by-twelve black-and-white glossy to her chest.

Renie agrees, though secretly she thinks the teen pop star bears an uncanny resemblance to Erica herself—the same brown, well-coiffed hair, the same narrow waist and hips, though in the picture, Tony's are draped in powder blue satin trousers.

Erica's also the first person Renie has ever met who's going to have a nose job. Despite her all-American looks, Erica has a slightly beaked nose, so her parents promised she could have the surgery in lieu of a Sweet Sixteen. Her name already resides on the waiting list of the best plastic surgeon in Manhattan. Still, three years is a long time to wait, and every few minutes Renie catches Erica staring at her own nose, which is small and pert and straight. Erica's envy of Renie's nose heartens Renie tremendously.

Erica is also the first person Renie knows who wears a M.I.A. bracelet.

"I have my own soldier," Erica says proudly, showing her the bulky silver bracelet engraved with a missing man's name. Despite its size, Renie thinks it looks quite elegant on Erica's thin tan wrist. "He's lost somewhere in the jungle."

"Where?" Renie asks.

"In Vietnam. From the war, you know."

Renie thinks about what she knows, trying to remember what she may have read about Vietnam in her seventh-grade Weekly Reader. She is confused because the adults said when Nixon got elected the war would end. But how can you end a war that was never really a war?

Then there is Patty Hearst, who Renie has not read about in her Weekly Reader but every kid knows about just the same. Patty Hearst was kidnapped earlier in the year, and at school they kept holding assemblies about not talking to strangers and never getting into the car of someone your parents didn't approve, though all the kids knew that Patty was taken right from her own home. Now Patty Hearst carries a gun—Renie saw it on television—and dresses in camouflage, robbing banks for something called the Symbionese Liberation Army.

Renie bets Patty was scared when she was kidnapped, but she can't help wondering too what it must be like to have such an exciting life, to carry a gun and be able to assume a new identity. Renie can't figure it all out, but her dad says these are sad and dangerous times. Renie rolls the phrase around in her head. Dang-er-ous.

So on the day that Mr. and Mrs. Saunders come to play pinochle, Erica comes along too.

"Nobody's going to bother you in the basement," Renie's mother says. "You and Erica can have a long play-date, a chance to really get to know each other."

Renie's basement is large and damp, covered with cold black tile, and is empty save for a washer and dryer and sink, an ironing board, a round white water heater hooked up to a series of noisy pipes, an old sagging day bed which serves as storage for a set of discarded luggage, and a group of warped wooden cabinets containing Renie's toys and board games.

The girls play Mousetrap, but when Renie manages to make the plastic yellow tub fall on Erica's mouse for the third time, Erica stands up from the tile floor, carefully brushing any dust from her Jordache jeans.

"I'm bored," Erica says. "I know, let's play photographer and model."

"We have some old dress-up clothes in one of the cabinets."

"Dress up is for babies," Erica says.

"Then how do you play?"

"Well," Erica says, slowly, "let's find a place for you to sit down and pose. I have a camera."

Erica walks over to her small blue-and-pink madras canvas bag and pulls out a new Polaroid. "I got this for my birthday last week. The pictures develop as soon as you take them."

Erica has been planning this, Renie thinks. She had a cool toy and wanted to show it off, but only when the time was right. Erica is always one step ahead of her, always has impeccable timing. Renie both hates and admires Erica for this.

There, in the dark dampness of the basement, tucked away underneath the stairs, surrounded by discarded luggage, and lying on the moldy, saggy day bed, well hidden behind the old giant water heater that gives off a thin aura of warmth as it speeds water through the pipes, Erica explains the game. "Put yourself in sexy poses, like the women in Playboy."

"I've never seen Playboy."

"You be the photographer first and I'll show you what I mean."

Erica gives Renie the camera. It feels bulky in her hand and doesn't look anything like the camera Dad uses. She's so busy trying to figure out which part of the black square box is the lens and which part the viewfinder that she's slightly startled to see

Erica already in her pose: hands up to her hair, head cocked to the right, legs spread open wide, so Renie can see the thick seams of her jeans where they meet at her crotch.

"Are you taking the picture?" Erica asks.

"I took it," Renie says, nervously. But her fingers shake when she pushes the black button on the camera, and no photo emerges.

"Talk to me, call out to me, tell me how you want me to pose."

"I don't know how to do this," Renie snaps.

"Oh, come on! All right, all right. You pose and I'll take the pictures."

Renie reluctantly moves back towards the bed. She lies down on it and stretches out in what she assumes is a seductive pose. She tries hard to remember how she has seen women do it on TV in the old black-and-white movies, the moon shining perfectly upon Jane Russell's luminous face as she lies back in a haystack, playfully throwing a piece of hay at the man off screen. The camera pans over full round breasts pressed tight against the fabric of her peasant dress to end with a close-up of her long creamy white legs. Or she is Jean Harlow lying languidly on a couch in a beaded dressing gown. She tries to imagine herself dressed all in silk, the material draped between her limbs, but she is acutely conscious of the rattling pipes, the smell of dust and mold rising from the day bed, and the fact that the only bulk rising from her chest comes from the white tank undershirt she wears beneath her cotton blouse.

"Stretch out, arch your back or something," Erica says. "No, not like that, you look so stiff."

As Erica approaches, Renie gets up to let Erica have her turn.

"No, silly," Erica says and pushes her back onto the couch. "You look dumb, just lying there like that. Look, why don't you put one hand behind your head and then place the other down by your hip, like this."

Erica takes Renie's right hand and places it. Then she stands up, walks back a few feet, and looks through the lens of the camera. "Smile," she says.

Renie tries to smile, but she can still feel the heat of Erica's flesh where she touched her. She recalls suddenly what it felt like to dance around nearly naked in the grass skirt.

"Why don't you show a little skin?" Erica suggests.

"What?"

"You know, unbutton the top of your blouse."

Renie looks down at her light blue cotton blouse with the lapel collar that comes to a point just below her neck. In the shadows of the basement, the tiny white buttons look almost translucent. Renie already has the top one undone. "It is."

Erica sighs and walks back over. She sits down and reaches for Renie's blouse. "Like this, silly," she says, and slowly undoes the rest of Renie's buttons.

Renie's heart starts to pound as Erica rearranges her blouse. She feels Erica's warm hands on the nape of her neck, draws in a deep breath as Erica's fingers run over her collarbone. Suddenly, Erica moves her hand down Renie's clavicle, slides it underneath her thin cotton undershirt and comes to rest on one of Renie's breasts. Renie can scarcely breathe. She closes her eyes while Erica strokes the brown circle and nipple and Renie feels the sensation all the way down to her belly. Erica has both hands on her breasts now, as Renie slowly begins to wriggle with pleasure.

She feels her nipples harden and rise. The sensation is too much for her. She opens her eyes in surprise. Her body is trembling.

Click. Click. And Erica straddles over her, taking Renie's picture as she squirms and moans. Click. Click. Renie hears the camera whir and sees the photo slide out from the bottom of the machine. Then she feels Erica's warm silky hand move down past her belly button and slip past her jeans towards the elastic of her underpants.

Frightened, Renie hardens her face, ready to throw her stare, the one she learned back in the fourth grade from Caroline Roth to ward off danger, but that she's since perfected and made her own. It's a sort of combination stare-glare that consists of jutting her chin out, tightening her mouth, nose and cheeks and hardening her eyes until they shine like cut amber. She aims for a sere, fierce, poisonous gesture that cannot be mistaken for anything else. A stare that can peel the skin off a plum, curdle milk, cause islands to collide. Like a poison dart from an Amazon blowgun felling prey in a single shot, it's the look that kills.

But suddenly she can't do it. The stare is gone. Instead, her eyes lock on Erica's and they look at each other face-to-face, naked, raw, as if seeing each other for the first time.

"You want me to, don't you?" Erica says.

"What?" Renie quivers.

"You want me to touch you... down there." Erica wriggles her fingers on Renie's lower belly, as if to remind Renie that her fingers are everywhere, can do anything. As if Renie doesn't already feel as though she is going to explode, as though her world hasn't gone topsy turvy and the only thing that matters is the heat of Erica's hand on her flesh.

Click click.

"I...no," says Renie.

"Say you want me to. I know you do. Say it. Just say it." Erica's voice grows thin and hard, more urging.

Renie turns her face from Erica, pushes the camera away and gets up from the couch. "I don't want to play anymore," she says.

They stand only a few feet away from each other, but to Renie that distance seems way too far. She craves Erica's coming back to her, having Erica run her long, delicate fingers back over her flesh, so she can again experience that dark, sharp longing.

Then she looks at Erica's lips and realizes she has absolutely no desire to kiss her. In fact, if all of Erica except those long fingers that stroked her breasts a few minutes ago would instantly disappear, she'd be more than happy.

"Girls, girls, what are up to?" Renie hears Dad's voice calling down to them.

Erica and Renie spring even farther apart. "Nothing!" Renie yells up.

The two girls right the few clothes that have gone awry and rush to the foot of the stairs. Though Renie knows what she and Erica have done together is part of the great secret she's just starting to unravel, now that the game has stopped, looking up at her father, she simply feels naughty.

"Your mother wants you to come upstairs. The Saunders are leaving. Come up and say goodbye like young ladies."

The girls ascend the stairs, Renie in the lead. Halfway up, she hears Erica hiss, "chicken." Renie turns back to look at her friend. Erica nudges the back of her knee. "Hurry up," Erica says. "My parents are waiting."

Later that night, Renie discovers Erica has snuck the photos into Renie's room. Perhaps it was when she picked up her coat where it lay on Renie's bed that she planted them. When Renie pulls back the covers, she finds three photos of herself lying on her pillow. There's nothing sexy about it. Her mouth is open, her eyes no more than slits. She looks like a fish out of water, gasping for breath, uncomfortable and strange. She can see every pore and her nose is bulbous—Erica has done it on purpose, made her look gross, obscene. She has the goods on Renie now. And what about the rest of the photos? Renie tries hard to remember how many clicks of the camera she heard. And what if Erika actually took pictures of Renie's breasts? Did she?

Renie suddenly thinks she knows why Patty Hearst became a bank robber after she was kidnapped, because she would do anything, try anything, so as not to feel trapped, feel controlled as Renie feels at this moment.

Renie scurries about her room, searching for some way to discard the photos. She runs to the kitchen to the family junk drawer to fetch a pair of scissors. But she stops when she sees her mother sitting at the kitchen table doing the Times crossword.

"What are you doing up?" her mother says.

"Got homework to finish," Renie says slowly. "I need the scissors to cut out some news clippings for Social Studies."

"How many times have I told you not to leave your homework to the last minute?"

"Sorry."

"Well, get it done."

Renie reaches into the drawer and fishes the scissors out from the mess of Scotch tape and staples and index cards. She holds the closed blades tight in her palm so they don't inadvertently poke someone's eye out, like she's been taught. "'Night, Ma," she calls out and backs out of the kitchen.

"Don't forget to put those scissors back where you found them!"

Renie's heart beats loudly, feeling the metal's heaviness in her hand. She cuts each photo in half, then cuts the halves into strips until there's nothing left of the images. Then she takes an envelope from her light blue stationery set, places all the pieces inside the envelope and seals the flap shut. For safe measure, she writes a made-up name on the front of the envelope. She puts it in the very bottom of her wastebasket and covers it up with some rumpled loose-leaf. Then she climbs into bed.

She's safe.

Two minutes later she climbs back out of bed, turns the lights on and retrieves the envelope from the wastebasket. She hides it at the bottom of her sock drawer.

The next day at school, she feels as if her limbs belonged to someone else. No longer able to shoot her stare at will, she feels exposed, like all the kids can guess her secret simply by looking at her.

As soon as last period ends, Renie rushes towards the school pool for swim practice. She quickly changes into her bathing suit, then hurls herself into the pool, grateful for its familiarity. She swims laps, feeling her body coming back into itself, the steady rhythm of her breathing, the calming repetition as she raises first her right arm, then her left, to stroke through the water. She swims for a half-hour without stopping. Then she climbs out of the pool, and pulls off the bathing cap to free her hair, feeling the water rolling down her bare legs in rivulets. She wraps her towel around her shoulders and enters the girls' locker room, sated, happy.

As she heads towards the back, she sees Erica in the row of lockers before hers. Dressed in a short blue flannel skirt and matching sweater, Erica has one foot on the wooden bench, tying her sneaker. Two other girls stand alongside her, dressed the same way. On the floor, Renie notes a mass of blue-and-white pom poms. They are getting ready to cheer at the boys' JV soccer meet.

Don't look up, Renie prays. Don't look up. But Erica does. The room is so still that Renie can hear the sound of her own blood as it rushes to her face. Erica looks at Renie quickly, then switches legs on the bench and begins tying her other sneaker. Renie dashes into the next row, her heart pounding.

"Who was that?" Renie hears one of the other girls ask.

"Who cares?" Erica says, raising her voice slightly, making sure Renie catches it. "She doesn't even wear a bra."

"A regular ironing board," the other girl agrees.

"Like, du-uh," chimes the second one.

The three girls break into peals of laughter. Renie sits down on the bench before her locker, squeezing her hands between her two legs as if that will stop them from trembling. Then she steps to the nearest mirror. Concentrate. If you concentrate really hard you can throw them the stare, go back out there eyes blazing, Patty Hearst with her gun. Concentrate.

She screws up her face, tries to harden her eyes; but it reminds her too much of the photos Erica took. Shivering in her wet bathing suit, she stands powerless before the mirror long after she hears the girls leave, their pom-poms swishing.

KARMA

By Na'amah Segal

Joel woke from his drugged stupor slowly, drool on his chin. He saw a soldier sitting across from him, reading from a file. The soldier was dressed in military fatigues. The colors could have been a dusty brown but with only a single overhead light shining, his blurred vision was playing tricks on him. Dressed with precision, his immaculate uniform displayed no rank or station, no name, no identifiers whatsoever. The man was in his mid-thirties, a high and tight of light brown hair, soft blue eyes, tan skin, and he needed a shave. He wore a thick headset that wound up to a port in the wall behind him. It dawned on Joel; they were in a helicopter.

He had no idea how he had gotten there. The last thing he remembered, he was in a cage, watching a sixty inch television playing an hour long video of his life's exploits. Every dirty deal, bad stock sold, back alley bargain, dirty politician bought, every mistress, every cruel act he had committed against his wife and the world, captured in an exhaustive, soundless vignette, playing on repeat. They had starved him; no one spoke to him for days despite the begging and threats.

Seeing his captive alive, the man closed the file and put it in his briefcase. He smiled warmly. Moving, he placed a headset on Joel's head. "Good morning sunshine. You're probably wondering what's going on. Firstly, in case you didn't notice, you're gagged and bound. I find it easier to travel that way. Secondly, allow me to introduce myself. My name is Hayden. I'm here to take you to your destination." Joel was shocked. The bastard was smiling at him. Joel muffled an angry response. Hayden reached over and removed the gag, then sat back down.

"Where are you taking me?" Joel asked weakly, his stomach screaming from hunger. Almost as though he read his mind, Hayden pulled out a small, bright, juicy pomegranate from a nearby bag. Then, a bowl and towel emerged. Lastly, from behind his back, he retrieved a very large black knife.

"This is a K-Bar," Hayden began, displaying the knife clearly in the overhead light. It made Joel's blood run cold. The black blade shone brightly and Joel noticed an emblem of an eagle, trident, anchor, and rifle engraved upon it. "And this, as you know, is a pomegranate. I'm very hungry and didn't have a chance to eat before we left." He spoke as though to a student. His manner calm and deliberate, he laid the towel across his lap and cut six lines across the fruit, from pole to pole. "It's a strange clutch of circumstance that's gotten you into this predicament," he said. His voice hid a mild southern accent. It immediately irritated the captive. Moreover, Joel was annoyed by Hayden's avoidance in answering.

"See, I've been studying you Joel. Ever since I got hired for this job, I've been studying you. I wanted to know just what kind of *man*," he used the word with a tinge of contempt, "would do the things you've done, to your company, your employees, and especially to your wife." He split the pomegranate and turned the open half face-down into the bowl. Looking up, he stared at Joel, hearing his belly growl, seeing the fury his dark brown eyes. He was enjoying the simple act of torture. Without breaking eye contact, he gently wiped the long blade on the towel, leaving a blood red stain in its wake. He flipped the knife in his hand and grasped the blade, then proceeded to whack the pomegranate firmly so that the seeds would fall into the bowl. "You see, you're pretty famous, from what I hear. Big hedge fund manager, Forbes top 100 richest men on earth, campaign contributor for every shitty senator your state has produced in the last few years. Beautiful wife. Huge house. Jet. Two yachts.

Vacation home in Saint Barts. You seem to have everything, and yet you haven't even hit your forties." He turned back his attention and finished the job on the second half of the pomegranate. "But, see, I studied you. I know who you really are. That's the reason I agreed to do this job. I really want to see you pay."

Joel shifted uncomfortably. No one had ever described his life with such icy calculation. It resonated somewhere deep within and he did not like it. "I want to know where you're taking me."

Hayden began popping pomegranate seeds into his mouth. "To your destination, of course," he replied.

Joel seethed. "Tell me where we're going. You need to let me go."

Hayden sharply shook his head. "I did tell you, Joel and I am letting you go. I'm taking you to your destination." Seeds kept popping into his smiling mouth.

Exhaustion was overtaking Joel. He was hungry, dehydrated, and hated to admit it, but terrified beyond the telling of it. "Please," he finally succumbed. "Please just tell me what's happening."

As though waiting for the desperation to hit just the right octave, Hayden grinned. "Well, since you said please; I have a mission for you. You have two days to get from the drop off point to your rendezvous. When you meet your point of contact, you may want to be extra nice. Let's just say, you're going to have to prove your worth if you're going to get out alive."

Speeding along, the dawn was approaching in Joel's window, illuminating a bright green landscape of fields, forests, and rivers. It was so green it hurt to look at it. He had been kept in the cage so long, he had forgotten how beautiful colors could be.

Joel finally roused from his drowsy silence. "You can't do this. Let me go. There are people looking for me." The words sounded pathetic even to his own ears.

"Oh yes, you're right, they're looking for you; because they're paid to. No one likes you Joel. You should know that. You're a shit. I pity your wife actually. She seems really nice. She's stuck with you through all this too. She must really love you." Joel's fists curled in rage. The same thoughts had been running through his head for five days. He couldn't think about it. He had to survive this.

With that, the pilot's voice sounded through the headset. *"Approaching target. Four minutes."* Hayden nodded. "Copy that," he replied. Turning to Joel, he said "Well we're nearly there," as casually as could be. "Tell me Joel. Do you have kids?"

There was a pregnant pause. His wife had begged. He had demurred. For years, they had fought over the topic. He couldn't be a father. He wouldn't be a father. She was shattered. Now he would die without ever knowing what if. Soundlessly, he shook his head.

"Yeah. I didn't think so. It wasn't in my file," his voice trailed off. "I've got three myself. My wife," his eyes alight, "she runs a tight ship. But she was raised off the land. She's got those kids growing up right," chuckling, he reached into his chest pocket and retrieved a photograph. "The youngest one, she's a charmer, like her mother. Want to see?"

Joel couldn't control anger. Whether this man killed him or not, he no longer cared. "Goddammit!" he screamed. "I don't give a shit about your family! Tell me what the hell is going on right now!"

The smile vanished from Hayden's mouth. Eyes turning cold, he slid the photo back in his pocket. Joel was panting. Suddenly, Hayden was all business. "Well, since you've decided not to show those manners you paid so much for, I guess I'll just brief you before the drop." He moved so quickly. He stood and moved past Joel, reaching to the door of the helicopter. He threw it open, letting huge gusts of cold wind fill the cabin. The sun had risen, golden light covering the earth.

"You see that?" Hayden pointed down below. A river rushed directly beneath them. "It flows north south. You're going to want to follow that." The sound of his voice was drowned out by the wind. He was shouting. "It's a beautiful sight but, don't drink the water." He looked down on Joel, eyes locked. "You have forty eight hours to reach your rendezvous point. Follow the river for about twenty clicks north. You'll see a big field on the western bank. Wait for sunrise on the third day. Hopefully you won't miss your ride."

Joel leered at the man, his captor. "You're just going to leave me in the middle of the fucking woods? What the hell is wrong with you?"

Hayden spoke then, chilling Joel to his bones. "Beautiful sunrise isn't it? You never notice the little things when you're so big, huh? Bet you've missed a lot of little things in your pursuit of power. I bet you didn't notice the pack on the floor here? It's got enough food and water to get you twenty clicks and not freeze to death from exposure. I recommend you hold on tight."

"*Thirty seconds to drop.*" The pilot's voice interrupted the exchange.

Joel was silent. He didn't know what to say; the truth rang louder than the river. Hayden spoke one final time. "I know one other thing you didn't notice, you scumbag," Hayden said with disgust, "the paracord wrapped around your waist. You're clueless Joel. Now you're going to get one final shot. Let's see if the bludgeoning of chance leaves you unafraid." With a grin on his lips, he stepped back, swiftly ripping the headset from Joel's head. His knife came out of nowhere and, in a flash, Joel's bonds were broken. Bracing himself against the ceiling, with one swift kick to the chest, Hayden launched Joel out of the helicopter.

He remembered falling. It was so fast. He watched Hayden's face grow smaller and smaller as he plummeted from above. The next thing he felt was a horrible snap as he reached the end of his rope and dangled above the riverbank. He looked up. Hayden was laughing. He was holding the bowl of pomegranate seeds. A sardonic grin crossed his face. He reached down below him to the anchor hook that held Joel's rope. Brandishing his blade, he cut the rope and Joel fell about ten feet, landing in the fetal position on the hard riverbank. Pain struck his side, his head ached sharply. In seconds, he started as the pack landed only feet away from his head. He managed to look up before the bird flew away. As he did, pomegranate seeds fell from the sky, landing like blood droplets all around him. Then Hayden was gone. He was alone.

Though he could barely move, Joel managed to gather his wits and got up. He scrambled for as many seeds as he could grasp, exploding sweetness into his dry mouth. He ripped the pack open, finding supplies neatly tucked within. He found the compass and located north. He was not a stupid man. Twenty clicks, the captor had told him. That meant more than ten miles north. He strapped the pack to his back and was on his way, aching but thrilled to be free and feel the cool air in his lungs.

Two days had passed longer than he had wished. He slept shivering in the cold, not daring to start a fire for fear he would attract some undesirable who might want to ransom him further. No, he thought, his only shot was to play this game and find a way out. On day three, he had stumbled, several hours before dawn, to an open field on the western side of the river. Realizing he was at his destination, he collapsed among the tall grasses and slept.

An old pickup truck woke him. He heard it coming, saw the sun high enough overhead to define the horizon. He waited in the grass to see an old rusted truck pull up from a road the darkness had hidden. It stopped not too far away and a slender woman emerged wearing worn overalls, a flowered button up blouse, old boots, and a straw hat.

"I know you're out here, Joel Cossini. You better wake up and get in this truck or I'm leaving." She climbed up and sat on the roof of the truck, legs dangling over the bed, slicing up a peach with a pocket knife. Joel stood, pack in hand, trying to brush the dirt and twigs from his hair. He walked towards her. They locked eyes, her strong grey eyes meeting his uncertain brown ones.

"You're my ride?" he asked.

"Yep. Nice to meet ya," she said clearly in a deep southern drawl, a slice of peach slipping into her mouth.

"Where are we going?" he asked.

"Home," she replied. "My home. There's three rules you need to know. One, do as I say no matter what, even if you don't understand why. Two, respect my home and everything in it. Three, you leave your anger here, never let it cross my threshold." She finished the peach and tossed the pit to the ground, rubbing her hands clean on a handkerchief which she then stuffed back into the chest pocket of her overalls. "If you break my rules Joel," she said, never taking her eyes from his. "No one will ever find you. Conversely, if you work hard, you *will* get out of here."

Joel was not willing to relinquish his control any further. He could take this woman in a fight. He would take her truck, find a town, get directions, and go home. He sneered at her.

"What the hell makes you think I'm going to do anything you tell me? What's to stop me from just killing you and taking your truck? You're nothing to look at. Your hands are so small I bet they couldn't even fit around a gun."

In the blink of an eye, she was on him, sprinting off the truck-bed, pouncing on his chest like a lioness and knocking the wind entirely out of him. His eyes were wide in fear. Hers were calm but bright. She had done this once or twice before. One knee in his chest, the other boot shoved up into his armpit. Her handkerchief dangled near his nose; it smelled of peaches and he stunk of fear. Like lightning, she brandished her knife, which was much larger up close. She slid it under his jaw, piercing his skin slightly.

Her breathing was fast but even. "My hands are small, I know. But they're not yours, they are my own. My knife can do any job I hand it. If you want to eat, shower, and sleep someplace out of the rain, you best cooperate Joel. I'm not here to hurt you; I'm your only shot."

She instantly got off him, slid the knife into an unseen pocket, and held out her hand to him. He had to decide. She could have killed him. She didn't. Humiliated, he accepted her hand and she jerked him effortlessly to his feet. She was stronger than she looked. They both got in the truck.

"Gotta empty your cup first Joel, if you're going to refill it," she said.

He got the message.

He was glad he hadn't stolen her truck; he would have gotten lost within minutes. Hills, valleys, lush vegetation, and nothing but rough dirt roads for miles. He counted one sign the entire time and it read, "No trespassing." He was so tired, he blinked and they arrived. The jolt of the rocky stone bridge startled him. He looked up as they pulled up to an impressive two-story farm house and nearby barn. Upon the porch were three girls, sitting and waiting. The moment they saw him, the three stood up and went inside. Each one waited her turn to remove her shoes before entering.

When they arrived, the woman got out first. She began to walk around towards the house. Joel found his voice then. "Hey, um, excuse me," he attempted being polite; he thought he failed. "I don't know you're name." Laying a single foot on the steps, she turned to him and responded.

"My name is Korrine. Everyone calls me Kori. Take off your shoes before you enter my house."

He obliged and followed after her, feeling suddenly naked. As he bent down and removed his shoes, he became conscious of how dirty he really was. Further embarrassment mounting, he set down his pack outside and crossed the threshold.

Her voice rang in his mind.

One, do as I say no matter what, even if you don't understand why.

Two, respect my home and everything in it.

Three, you leave your anger here, never let it cross my threshold.

The house smelled like herbs, wood smoke, honey and fresh bread. His gut twisted from hunger and worry. The large main room was neat as a pin, homey and inviting. Kori walked into the kitchen which was visible from the great room, assisting the oldest girl in preparing something. The middle girl was setting a tray with cups. The youngest was playing on the floor. Her toy of choice seemed to be a child-sized measuring scale with tiny weights that could sit on either side. She was weighing blocks and marbles. She looked up with warm blue eyes.

Kori approached with a towel and a pile of clothing. "Shower is in the back. Water's hot. Come back when you're clean and you can eat."

He followed her instructions. In the back of the house was a large Victorian bathroom, complete with claw-foot tub. He scoured himself with homemade soap full of oatmeal and smelling of honey lavender. He emerged after a long time, clean and wearing fresh clothes. He returned to the great room and found Kori waiting for him. He walked slowly up, his body aching everywhere, stomach in knots.

"Joel, these are my daughters," she motioned towards the three standing girls. "The oldest is Athena, she's twelve. The middle one is Melissa, she's ten. The youngest is Deborah, she's six." Each girl nodded at him, displaying varying genetics but all looking like their mother. The youngest smiled at him and plopped right back down to play with her scales. "Come sit down. I bet you're hungry."

He nodded. The table was beautifully set before him. On a white tablecloth, fresh bread, hot coffee, a large scoop of mashed potatoes, a slice of ham steak, two scoops of fresh green beans, and a thick slice of cornbread with honey butter dripping from it. He nearly forgot himself as he ate. Kori came up behind him once, making him freeze, and laid her small hand on his shoulder. "Mind you don't eat too fast Joel. It would be a shame to throw all this back up." He took the hint and slowed down, reveling in the meal.

After a full belly, he stood up and the middle child Melissa took his plate to the kitchen. Athena and Deborah were sitting near the fireplace working with yarn. Kori handed him a blanket and pillow. "There's a cot outside on the porch. It's warm enough at night, you shouldn't take a chill. It's screened in so the bugs will leave you be," she said as she walked him out onto the porch. Turning to face him, she placed her hand on his hand. Her eyes searched him like an arrow to its target. He felt naked again. "Tomorrow morning you'll chop wood and haul water for me. Next day, you do the same. And the day after that. And the day after that. And if you can keep up with me and my girls for seven days, then I'll promote you to run my trade up to the neighbors and back. Let you earn enough for a bus ticket home."

He nodded. Taking her leave, he turned and looked out onto the forest. He had no idea where he was. Her truck had no plates. There were no distinguishing features anywhere that he could find. And the girls weren't talking. They were stoic but polite. No, he supposed he would have to cooperate if he were to get out of there. He laid down on the cot, hoping nothing crawled up and bit him. At that moment, reality struck him. He had nothing. Literally. Nothing. The food he was given was a gift. The shower. The clothing. Even the ride to Kori's house. All freely given. He hadn't even said thank you. She did not seem to enjoy keeping him there but she gave him quality food when she could have given table scraps. Exhaustion was setting in. He was too tired to be angry. His anger died in the woods. Sleep took him.

***

Joel's mouth was slack. He couldn't believe what she was telling him. He had just arrived by bus to Chicago. He had spent nearly twenty four hours traveling. He was exhausted. He hurt. He stunk. But he also felt a sense of rebirth he never thought would be his. He had earned that ticket.

Every strike of the axe. Every bucket of water. Each basketful of loaves of bread or jars of honey or skeins of yarn he toted back and forth for the women of the woods had earned him the money for a single ticket home. Within weeks, his strength returned and he felt alive. He had stopped caring about home, only remembering the wife he had failed, hoping she had forgotten him. He was happy being present. All he cared about was the work before him, about pleasing Kori, serving that family, those girls, who smiled at him shyly, who left him dandelion chains on his pillow, who balmed his hands when they bled. The resentment he felt the first few days faded. After some time, he accepted his circumstances, recognizing he was only there because his life had led him to be there, to be kidnapped, tested, and broken in order to be reforged. In this surrender, he found himself again. He wasn't even angry when Hayden drove up in his truck. The two men stared at one another and Hayden smiled, bending down to scoop up Deborah. He reached in his pocket and held out four hundred dollars. "That's enough to get you home. I'll drive you to the bus stop."

Joel simply nodded, lowering his head. It had been a test; his soul was at stake. For the first time in his memory, he had worked in service to others without concern for himself. He supposed that's why Hayden picked him up. The girls watched him on the porch as he left, Kori leaning against a post, slowly slicing up a peach. She nodded slowly at him. In that moment, he felt something he had never known: a job well done.

Now this woman before him, his wife's sister Katya, was sitting on his couch, smoking a cigarette and telling him, "Welcome home, asshole. How was your ordeal?" His jaw hit the floor. She knew.

"Where's Annushka," he asked. She took a long drag.

"Out. She doesn't know you're home yet. She doesn't know any of it." She stared at her brother-in-law. Understanding was dawning on Joel.

"You did this to me." His words were cold. She tapped the ashes of her cigarette onto a magazine with his face emblazoned upon it.

"Yes, Joel. I did." She stood up. She watched him, waiting to see his anger. But there was none. "I paid the team to snatch you, starve you, and deposit you some place where no one would ever find you, under explicit instructions not to release you unless *you earned it*. So yes, it was me. How does it feel, hmm?" She was overflowing in icy rage. She wanted him broken for all the things he had done to her sister over the years.

He inhaled slowly, feeling his new calluses rub together on his hands. "Before all this happened, I would have beat you with my own hands and had you arrested, escorted out of here, and told Annushka you had it coming. But," he sighed, "After everything that's happened, I feel like I don't even deserve to see her. I was a monster, Katya. I know why you did it. I know in my heart that I deserved it all, every minute of it. Please don't tell her I came home. She deserves a life without me." He lowered his head and walked out the door.

She stared. As a lawyer she was trained to spot a lie. There were none. He believed it all. He had been reborn.

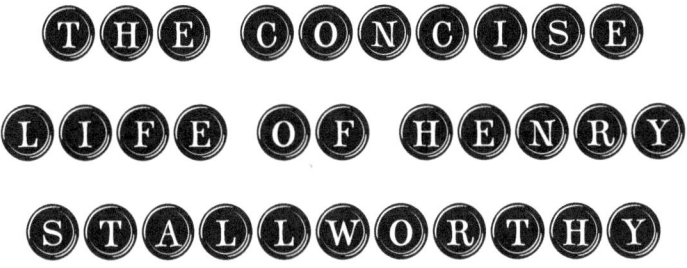

THE CONCISE LIFE OF HENRY STALLWORTHY

By Stephen McQuiggan

Five minutes after vomiting Henry was back at the bar with a pint in front of him. This was how life slipped you by, but he was so bored he hardly noticed anymore. He was on autopilot, asleep at the wheel, and heading for a crash that he welcomed in his heart. His death had become a fetish to him. Anything was better than merging with the faceless masses.

Only the constant drill of pain enriched his life and made him real. Sorrow and misery were the only highlights of his monochrome existence, the only bits worth taping. If life were a movie, he thought, you would watch it on fast forward yawning between the action scenes. Death was preferable.

But the bored lived a long time, each minute stretched to breaking point. The bored might well be immortal if they didn't kill themselves to liven things up. He was so weary of struggling through the clotted passage of his being. There had to be something more and he planned to drink until he found it.

He sipped his pint, feeling his stomach lurch as a vanguard of bile charged up his throat. "I wish you could just live the good bits," he said to the pale reflection in the mirror behind the optics. "The meaningful bits." Then he hurried to the toilets once more.

But when he opened the door, instead of urinals and an overpowering stench of bleach, he found himself in a small cramped office. The contents of his stomach retreated in surprise. A clerk, skinny as a bar of cheap rock, was scribbling away behind a desk. Henry could hear the "tut-tut" of his pen over the clone and drone of the photocopier. By the clerk's elbow, acting as a paperweight, was a picture of a woman without a face.

Henry was instantly wary of him, for he appeared more insect than human. He was afraid the clerk might touch him and that his touch would be the cold one he feared in the dead of night; the reason he couldn't sleep if all his limbs weren't covered. The clerk looked up as if he sensed he was being stared at. He looked tiny behind the black carapace of his desk.

"Mr. Stallworthy?"

Henry started. "How do you-"

"I won't be a moment. I just need your signature for our records."

"Signature? I don't understand."

"Don't worry, it's really just a formality. Your wish has already been authorised by the Board."

"My wish? Am I dead?"

The clerk laughed. "No sir, you are very much alive. How does it feel to be alive?"

Henry merely gawped in reply.

"If you would just sign here," the clerk tapped a piece of paper with his pen. "And here."

Henry scrawled his name feeling the clerk frown behind him at every incompetent stroke. He noticed that the little man reeked of Brylcreem even though he was completely bald.

"So what have I signed up for?"

"Why, the best bits Mr. Stallworthy. All the meaningful moments of your life with no filler in between. The meat without the bread."

"You're kidding me, right?"

The clerk gestured toward the door. "If you wouldn't mind sir, there are others waiting."

Henry left mumbling an apology. He found himself in a dark, narrow corridor whose far end was dimly lit by a tiny red door that was barely more than a slit. The shadows clung to it like matted hair. He walked slowly toward it, feeling his fear shiver around him. It looked like a cave where childhood monsters might lurk.

It was a squeeze to get through the tiny opening even though the sides were lubricated with some form of mucus. It hurt as he pushed, and he cried as he slipped through to the other side and found himself in a hospital room. He had no idea what was going on. He felt like a fly on a TV screen, surrounded by sights and sounds that made no sense.

A woman was writhing on the bed, screaming obscenities, grasping onto a man's hand so tightly she had drawn blood. The man looked trapped between illness and embarrassment. Underneath his pallid mask Henry recognised him; it was his father. And the swearing, sweating mess that clung to him was his mother.

"None too clever this birthing process," said the clerk from behind him. "Throws everything out of whack."

"What is this?"

"It's your birthday."

"My-"

But the clerk was gone. A baby yelled. He saw the child emerge, surfing on the tidal wave that gushed from his mother, a six pound pot roast erupting through the open window his mother spread from one world to the next. The doctor opened a window too; the noxious fumes accompanying its arrival were overwhelming.

They make you pay for such indiscretions. He remembered vividly the birth canal, as fetid and clotted as the one by Romannon Street; the terror as he hit vegetation. His first birthday, no cake, no candles, just blood and guts and tears; a prototype of all that would follow.

He looked at his small crying self. Such an ugly baby. He was just a short slap away from being thrown to an indifferent world, full of little miracles, bored to death of them. Why had they bothered? He had been an Elastoplast baby, used to cover the festering wound of his parent's marriage. He had failed miserably, something his mother pointed out to him on a daily basis.

The doctor held the dripping child aloft, a sacrificial lamb offered to a hungry God. The sight of blood on his mother's thighs, on his tiny arms and protruding belly made him cry. He had been sensitive from a tender age.

"It's a…" The doctor paused for the longest time and Henry felt the shame of the changing room return, "…a boy!"

The baby reached for the umbilical, tried to crawl back, intuitively aware he did not belong here, but the lifeline was cut and he was left stranded. They swaddled him in a blanket and presented him, a bouquet of pink steaming meat, to his mother. She clucked, turned her eyes in, mouthed nonsense words. It was then that Henry had had his first coherent thought: My mother is an idiot.

Enough. He squeezed back out the door, into the dim corridor, and found Sheba waiting for him. He had forgotten all about her and her gentle brown eyes. She'd been the only one who had ever been pleased to see him; how could he have forgotten her? She barked a greeting and Henry felt something inside him slip. His dad had always told him not to stick his toe into the bath plughole, told him it would suck him down with the water. Now here he was, on the other side, for Sheba had been dead for twenty years.

He had buried her at the bottom of the garden and he had talked to her every day. Of course, he had pretending to be weeding just in case his mother was watching him. You come for me when it's my time Sheba, he always told the little mound of earth before he left, and we'll be together forever.

"Are you my guide girl?"

Wagging her stumpy tail she bounded into a pillar of bright light barking for him to follow. He ran after her, crying "Stop!" for the last time she had bounded into the light it had been the headlamps of a Vauxhall Viva and her little body had crunched beneath the wheels.

He closed his eyes as he raced into the heart of the pillar. He felt a shower of insects crawl over his face, their hard pellet bodies scraping his skin. Their countless legs, barbed with coarse hair and dipped in dung, tickled his lips, and made him gag. He felt the jackboots of a superior race march over his flesh and he leapt from the light rubbing frantically at his skin in disgust.

He landed in a church filled with a few mumbling mourners.

"Bad turn out," said the clerk behind him. "I asked around but no one had anything really good to say about you, although the Reverend said you were held in high esteem and praised your whistling ability."

"Where am I?"

The clerk pointed to a coffin underneath the pulpit. "Why, it's your going away party Mr. Stallworthy."

No one was crying; that was disappointing. The small band of the mercy circus that had huddled under the Lord's cold roof were dry eyed and catatonically bored. In place of sobbing there was only a slight rustling and the occasional clink of a boiled sweet against false teeth.

Where are all my friends? He didn't recognise half the people here; they were far too old to be acquaintances. Who will lift my coffin then? No one here seemed fit enough. They seemed to be frozen in the act of queuing, not mourning. They were using his funeral as a dress rehearsal for their own. He turned to ask the clerk but he was nowhere to be seen.

In a small room to one side he saw a table filled with ham sandwiches and the realisation that he was overseeing his own death suddenly hit home. Ham sandwiches were the broken mirror, the number thirteen, the grim reaper of the food world; there could be no send off without them.

The lettuce and tomato were all show and the egg and onion would just repeat on you all day; you certainly didn't want to be trumping in a small room like that. No, the ham sandwich was the morbid snack of choice; crusts cut off, shaved like a marine, ready to kick the filling out of the Nancy boy cucumbers.

Henry watched as an old woman helped herself, the ham protruding from the bread like a tongue between dead lips, and washed it down with the obligatory strong tea. How can anyone eat when the air is filled with the nauseating stench of roses? And why in the hour of my own funeral can I only think of food; was there nothing more profound than Spam?

He watched his mother talking to Reverend Campbell, laughing at some weak joke he'd made. She'd always referred to him as a sanctimonious old hypocrite, yet here she was flirting with him over her son's body. She was wearing an awful green dress; in the midst of death, we are an embarrassment.

Henry walked up the aisle and looked at himself in the coffin. He looked young, he thought, too young. With his mouth glued shut, pursed like a pencil sharpener, and his suit and tie on he looked like a prefect. He looked like the kind of boy he would've picked on at school. In death, all things looked artificial, manmade; but Henry looked more real than he had ever felt. As a final insult they'd combed his hair wrong too.

116

He could not bear to look at the dummy in the casket any longer; leave it to God, he thought striding back down the aisle. Leave it to the great ventriloquist in the sky. He was sweating now, despite the chill air, and his sweat reeked of attar. He stopped a moment by the small garden of wreaths sprouting by the door. One spelt out SON in shiny plastic flowers; then, at last, someone cried.

Wiping the tears from his eyes Henry pushed through the heavy church door and found himself back in the clerk's cramped office. Stepping over the box-files that lay on the floor like homogenous headstones, he approached the odd little man who was still scribbling away.

"What am I doing back here?"

Looking up, the clerk spread his bony hands in sympathy. "You've had your quota Mr. Stallworthy."

"Two days? That's it?"

"I think you'll find it's three."

"I've had birth and death. I think you'll find that's only two."

"And you have today Sir. Making three. The magic number."

"What's today?"

"Today's the day you made your wish."

As Henry stared at him, he could feel his sickness return; a tendril of bile snaked up his throat.

"Who are you?"

The clerk smiled. "Just someone who made a wish. Someone like you." He gestured toward the door. "If you don't mind Sir, there are others waiting."

Henry left, barely making it out before emptying the contents of his stomach over his shoes.

Five minutes after vomiting Henry was back at the bar with a pint in front of him. This was how life slipped you by, but he was so bored he hardly noticed anymore.

DIAGNOSIS

By Bryn Fortey

Pictures at an exhibition. Jane Kavotny shivered. The gallery was cold, too cold, though it probably suited the series of anticipated death scenes the artist had produced for this particular show: ten for the pop singer Lucinda, ten concerning movie actor Jeff Halliday. Neither had actually posed for the paintings, but both had endorsed them after private viewings. Kavotny shrugged mentally, that had been their public posturing but she wondered what had been their inner feelings. She, personally, would not want to see her potential deaths splashed in larger-than-life and vibrantly coloured canvases. The artist, Leonard Sargasso, had talent, there was no denying that, but with a morbidity she did not appreciate.

"Jane, my dear, I'm late. Do forgive me."

She turned to face Dr. Parry.

"Have you had a first look?" he asked

Kavotny nodded. He had been seeking her company, and opinions, a lot lately. Either he valued her input, or she herself had become the focal point of one of his investigations.

"What did you think of the painting of Halliday as one with the twisted metal of the crashed helicopter?"

That caught her off guard a little. "You've seen them already?" she asked, surprised.

"Oh yes! Leonard Sargasso is…er…a friend of long standing. I was in the background when both the subjects had their personal introductions to the paintings. They both knew what Leonard was doing, of course, but their first look at such realistic representations was most interesting."

The hesitation intrigued her. Either it was genuine and his relationship with the artist depended upon interpretation, or it was a deliberate attempt to guide her in a direction that Parry felt unable to suggest himself.

A number of smartly attired mannequins had been placed throughout the gallery; some sitting, some standing, all posed in slightly different ways. The dead-studying-the-dead symbolism was too obvious, she thought. There had to be more subtle meanings, but at this moment in time Jane felt that she was being manipulated like a shop window dummy herself.

"I thought the idea was that we would compare our initial reactions," she complained, wondering how long she should stay before good manners dictated she could leave.

Whale songs for the broken-hearted. Alan Buxton never tired of listening to his recordings of male humpback whales. The plaintive sounds spoke of watery depths and moved him in ways very little else could. Sweet Gloria, the love of his life, had drowned at sea with others, and he hoped with all his heart that sad whale songs had accompanied their transition from life to death.

Dr. Parry had handed Buxton a small printed business card at the end of that week's group session. "Go to this gallery," he had suggested. "You have yet to challenge death face-to-face. The paintings currently on show might help you."

Miss Kavotny, who took notes during the sessions, stopped him as he was leaving. "Are you familiar with the work of Leonard Sargasso?" she asked.

"Leonard who?"

"Sargasso, the artist. It's an exhibition of his work the doctor wants you to visit."

Buxton shook his head. "Never heard of him," he replied. "I know nothing at all about art."

"Well, be warned, Mr. Buxton, his paintings do not make for easy viewing."

He remembered the brief conversation now, as he glanced at the programme purchased as he had entered the gallery. Ten paintings each, he read, featuring the images of Lucinda and Jeff Halliday in various death scenes. He had heard of her of course: Lucinda, the current pop sensation, more famous for her costumes than anything else. To the best of his knowledge, he had never actually heard her sing. The Halliday character was said to be an actor, but Buxton had not been to the cinema since losing Gloria, and even before that had only tagged along to see films of her choice.

The dummies were an initial shock; still, not breathing, but horribly lifelike at first glance. Only a closer examination revealed them to be manufactured. Buxton grimaced, trying to ignore the figures as he looked in turns at the paintings.

Most of the Halliday series portrayed him dying in action man settings: unopened parachute, crashed helicopter, mountaineering accident, and others, though there was also one showing him dead in a hospital bed. Those featuring the pop singer incorporated more fantasy elements, ranging from her being devoured by zombies to her corpse being attended by fairies. Whereas they were obviously very well painted, there was no hiding that, Buxton could not see that anyone would want to hang one on their living room wall.

The very last painting was of Lucinda being turned to stone by the Gorgon, but he didn't see that one. The canvas before it was a seascape of sorts, with the drowned pop singer sinking to oceanic depths. It hit Buxton like a hammer blow to the head and as he looked, staggered by the upswing of horror and grief brought bubbling to the surface of his mind, so the dead face morphed from the singer it was meant to be to that of the woman he had loved and lost.

His throat felt constricted, gasping for air, and his voice was dry and cracked. "Gloria!" he called out, and when he finally dragged himself away from the painting he found that the nearby mannequins had taken on her features too.

"Gloria," he repeated, this time in a whisper. Turning sharply, barely keeping his feet, almost falling, he rushed from the gallery and out into the horn and engine noises of a busy thoroughfare.

Sex dreams for sale. Dr. Parry had initially been a father figure for Jane Kavotny and she had experienced severe self-disgust when her feelings for him had taken on sexual overtones. Since he was such an expert in the theoretical needs of both the male and female, she granted him Casanova status, and the more she fantasised about him the less guilty she felt. In the end, the paternal viewpoint faded completely, but so did his sex-bomb standing.

Everything the doctor did had multiple reasons and seemed so planned. Jane wanted spontaneity. To be swept off her feet, to be surprised, even in her imagination. No, more than that: especially in her imagination. The darker and deeper layers of Jane's personal extravaganzas were for inward consumption only. Nothing intruded into the real world.

She had never seen the point in fantasising about singers or movie stars. Jane wanted the added thrill of genuine possibility, even while acknowledging she would never act on these secret desires. So when the good doctor fell out of favour, she cast around for a replacement, looking first at the male members of Parry's self-help groups.

The forlorn and wasted figure of Alan Buxton was an early possibility. Gaunt, troubled, pining for a lost love and unable to move on from her death. Jane pictured herself as the one woman capable of breaking him free from the crippling chains of loss that weighed him down. It was quite a satisfying dreamscape in that she cast herself in a Good Samaritan role, almost on a par with nurses and missionaries. But however illuminating it might be to be good, it didn't quite match the shivering excitement of a badass partner, and that made her look at Eric Landreth, a relative newcomer to Dr. Parry's circle of troubled souls.

Landreth, bristled with dark moods, a sense of resentment, and was troubled by acute anger issues. Jane felt a delicious thrill as she considered the violence that bubbled beneath his brooding exterior. She could see something of Emily Bronte's Heathcliff character about him. Cue Lucinda singing her cover version of Kate Bush's *Wuthering Heights* song, which in turn brought Saragossa's exhibition to mind. Eric Landreth could well be the only person she knew, apart from Dr. Parry, who might actually like the twenty paintings on show. She wondered if Alan Buxton had gone to the gallery and, if so, what his reaction had been?

Blues in the night. The Cool Spot was two evenings a week – Mondays and Tuesdays, traditionally quiet in the pub trade – in the upstairs bar of The Kings Head Tavern. Trad Jazz and Blues Bands pulled in the most punters and Swing Nights did okay, but Harry "Bugs" Bonney was committed to featuring jazz in all its shades and genres. He usually lost money on the Modernists, who had their followers but did not pick up as much passing trade as the others. That was fine though, it all evened out in the end, and Harry stayed true to his ideals.

Breathless was playing tonight, alto and tenor leads backed by double bass and drums. Not that a piano-less group was anything new; Gerry Mulligan was doing it back in the nineteen-fifties. These lads weren't bad though, making a good fist at reproducing the delicate traceries of counterpoint that Mulligan and Chet Baker had pioneered back in the day. The audience was small but enthusiastic, and Bonney could live with that.

"The boys are playing well tonight, Bugs," called someone as the group finished their deconstruction of a standard blues motif.

His surname being so close to that of the well-known cartoon rabbit, he had been nicknamed Bugs from schooldays on.

"Where's the action, Bugs?" asked Eric Landreth.

Bonney knew it went on, but did his best to discourage it. "Nothing going on here," he replied, knowing it to be a lie but wishing it were true.

"Uppers, downers, all over towners; where's the Dealer, the man to see," recited Landreth, paraphrasing lines from an old poem he had read years before in a small press magazine.

"You're always throwing that quote around!" Bonney was hoping to move the conversation on. "Who was the writer?"

"Dylan Thomas?"

"No, man, it wasn't anyone you would have heard of."

That one suggestion had exhausted Bonney's knowledge of Welsh poets. "Sounds more like Lou Reed lyrics than a poem to me," he said, irritably, but Landreth had already moved on, circulating the small crowd as he tried to find someone he could score from.

The house on the hill. Oakwell had been in the Parry family for generations. It boasted fantastic views of the surrounding town and a banqueting hall large enough to hold dances. It must have been an imposing building in its day, set in spacious grounds and lording it over the immediate area. Dr. Parry's father had often reminisced about the big parties and dances held there when he was still only a boy. "Ah, Trevor, they were really grand affairs," he would say. "I would creep from my bed and sneak a look at everything that was going on; such laughter and colour. Your grandmother was an absolute beauty,

124

my boy, and everybody said what a lucky chap your grandfather was."

But that was then, and this was now.

Bad investments and a conviction that nothing would ever change both contributed to what started as a gradual decline in the family fortunes, and ended with an almighty rush. By the time Trevor Parry returned to Oakwell to bury his father and accept his inheritance, the grounds were overgrown and the house was in a dilapidated state of disrepair. As a single man whose every thinking moment was devoted to his profession, he tried to keep tidy the few rooms he used and let the rest continue to deteriorate. Such mundane things were of no interest to him at all. Only his investigations mattered.

Leonard Sargasso, he decided, could be put down as a partial success. A depressive drunk who no longer lifted a paintbrush. When they had first met more than a decade previously, the artist would always look on the dark side, but was drink-free now and had re-established himself as a painter of note. Dr. Parry had not seen Leonard for the last couple of years and had been quite touched by the level of involvement his former patient had given him for his latest exhibition.

As he had known it would, the painting of Lucinda drowning had sent Alan Buxton spiraling downwards. He needed to turn off the whale songs and face the reality of death, and maybe this shock tactic might do the trick. Either way, Dr. Parry would pick up interesting data, and that was always his prime objective. The prim and proper Miss Kavotny, for instance, had provided him with so much information when being hypnotised, sessions she personally had no memory of.

Dr. Parry smiled, maybe a little ruefully. Jane had got it so completely wrong when granting him super stud status. It had been a relief, almost, when she had lost interest in him and started to consider other options. It was just as well she only wanted fantasy lovers. Eric Landreth would almost certainly show cruel and nasty tendencies in a real life situation.

A, to B, to C, to D. One thing often led to another. Dr. Parry visited The Cool Spot early, hoping to pick up information regarding Landreth's drug use. The man himself denied he was still a user, but addicts were notorious liars. As it happened, the promoter fellow, Harry Bonney, was more than willing to chat. He obviously didn't like Eric so didn't hold back, providing the doctor with a wealth of additional data, and also enabling a file to be opened on him too. Bonney was an interesting jumble of psychiatric jigsaw pieces and Parry could see many challenges in trying to make them all fit.

Jane Kavotny, Alan Buxton, Eric Landreth, and now Harry Bonney; there were others on his books, but these were the really interesting ones. Parry wondered if a more informal setting might pay dividends. Maybe a dinner party at Oakwell? The more he thought about it, the more the idea appealed.

A set menu. The large banqueting hall, with its long central table: dusty, unkempt, unused, reminded Harry Bonney of Miss Havisham's wedding reception room in Dickens' *Great Expectations*. What potential though! Tidied, modernised, repaired, a lick of paint alone would work wonders, and he could see himself putting on some great jazz gigs here.

Dr. Parry had invited Harry earlier than the others, hoping some time alone would help fill in the background information so important for both diagnosis and treatment. Bonney smiled slyly, secretly amused that the doctor thought he could keep his motives hidden. Maybe it worked with the others, but not with smart-arsed Bugs. "Quite some place," he said.

"It was once!" Parry had enjoyed giving his guest a guided tour. "The decline started in my grandparent's time, according to my father." They had returned to his living quarters and he poured a glass of beer for them both.

Bonney toyed with his drink, knowing that soon he would have to come to a decision. This doctor fellow was no fool, smarter than most, but not quite as clever as he thought himself to be. He had spotted Bonney's unusualness, for which he deserved full credit, but was confident of keeping his own strange tastes secret.

Ha! Bugs Bonney was as well versed at reading the signs as Dr. Parry. The difference being that the doctor did not realize it. He glanced at a clock ticking away on the room's mantelpiece. If he was going to act, it had better be now.

"What's up Doc?" asked Bonney, putting on his best Bugs Bunny voice.

"Pardon?"

As Parry turned towards him, Bonney struck his forehead as hard as he could with a metal hammer he had taken from a bag he had brought with him. Stunned, probably fully unconscious, his feet were expertly tied and he was hung, head down, against a door, with the rope going over and being knotted around the opposite side's handle. Placing a bowl from the kitchen under the doctor's head, he cut his throat, severing the arteries to facilitate blood removal from the incapacitated body. While that was happening he cut away Parry's clothing.

"Were you going to eat me or cure me, doctor?" murmured Bugs, taking down the slaughtered cadaver. It was time to dress the flesh.

"It takes one to know one," he said, continuing the one-sided conversation while first of all making the primal cuts, with minimum wastage of course. "You were so pleased with yourself, spotting my cannibal tendencies, that you missed realizing that I could see the same in you."

Next, he trimmed the primal cuts, in preparation for cooking. The other three: Eric Landreth, Alan Buxton and Jane Kavotny were in for a special treat tonight. Bugs just about had time to tidy up the place while the meal was cooking, and then the other guests would be arriving.

THE RIDE

By Rob Nicholson

Life is behind me. Blue sky. The smell of fresh cut grass. The random neighborhood sounds like dogs barking and children playing, are all behind me. There is no turning back. In front of me is something much more bleak. A view that sends an unease through my body.

Low lying hills drift off into a foggy distance with no signs of life. The landscape is sprinkled with just a handful of dead trees. Their leaf-less branches like skeletal limbs reaching up towards a brown overcast sky. Scattered patches of yellow grass rest motionless waiting for a breeze that may never come.

There's a group of at least a dozen of us. Their names and faces are unknown to me. How we got here and where we're going is just as unclear. I see a set of narrow railroad tracks on the ground before me. They appear more like the tracks from a small scale train or a roller coaster rather than something that might actually carry a large freight engine. The tracks curve towards a dark stone archway set in the hill before us. There seems to be movement in the darkness of the tunnel. It stops the moment I see it, almost as if whatever it was that was moving realized that it had been seen. I stare into the black trying to catch more movement. Something is definitely there staring back at me. I am snapped out of my daze as a train suddenly appears to my right coming to a stop just a few yards away. The train could of easily have come from some children's train park with its miniature diesel engine and single person passenger cars open to the sky above. But after a closer look I realize that no child would ever have willingly ridden a train like this one.

The front of the train seems to form a face with a threatening smile. Its two lights are like eyes staring ahead daring anyone to block its path, and its steel grill like sharp teeth ready to swallow anyone unfortunate enough to do so. The colorless paint faded and flaking off like a cancerous skin. A tall thin pale man dressed in a black suit and top hat, looking more like a mortician than a train conductor, sits atop the engine. His long legs straddling its sides. He is up and off of the train moving towards the group of us. Once he's closer I can feel there is an evil about him and I'm instantly aware of the fear in the small crowd around me. He simply informs us that we are next.

The group is larger than the train has cars, so the man begins to hand pick the first group of riders. I am the first one selected as the man is suddenly before me grabbing my wrist.

He breathes, dips and then the train settles into a straight downward path. Occasional flashes of small caverns and other tunnels shooting off in different directions break up the long decline as we gradually pick up more speed. The air blasting my face getting hotter by the second. Screams from off in the distance and from nearby tunnels continue to echo off the walls.

The next thing I know, the train has rounded a corner into the center of an enormous cavern that is lit by molten lava from below. The train is you.

His hand is cold and seemingly steals the life out of my arm. His eyes stab straight into my heart, taking away any sense of resistance. Instinct would have me run, but here I am powerless. I have no choice but to obey. He quickly moves through the rest of the group picking the remaining riders behind me. We then begin to move towards the train getting ready to embark. The cars are being filled faster than I can find an empty seat. I move towards the rear of the train to find the last car empty. The seat is more like a small bench with its ancient darkened wood worn smooth from countless riders. I sit down and after a quick search realize that there is no seat belt. I fight desperately with the panic building inside me.

With no notice, the train lurches forward. Picking up speed we pass quickly through the tunnels opening and into the darkness. My last sight of the outside world is a pair of stone gargoyles perched on either side of the top of the archway. Like watch dogs to the gates of hell. Their cold empty eyes staring directly at me as their fanged smiles seem to say in unison, "have a nice trip!" From somewhere distant I hear maniacal laughter.

Once inside the darkness, the train almost immediately drops down a steep hill. I instinctively stretch my legs out in order to try and wedge myself securely in my seat. I reach out to grab on to any part of my car as the train continues to pick up speed. My hands find a bar in front of me that I grasp tightly just as the train turns sharply to my right. It continues on that course for barely seconds then jerks back to the left following a long sharp curve. The sound from the train making a roar that echoes off invisible walls.

The ride briefly reminds me of a time on a similar ride as a young teenager on a trip to a family amusement park in Florida. The ride being a space themed roller coaster housed inside of a large futuristic looking building. It threw you around in near total darkness, with campy disco music and glowing stars on the ceiling to make it look as if you were flying in outer space. The ride was certainly fun and exhilarating, but here being a lifetime later there is very little to compare it to. Instead of joy and excitement, the darkness now only brings fear and dread. Then with the image of the pale man still in my head, the fear morphs into terror.

After speeding over a small hill, I can feel the train slow and then come to a complete stop. There's a short pause and as we begin moving again, a loud metal clicking can be heard somewhere ahead of me. It sounds like a chain somewhere beneath the train has grabbed a hold and is pulling the train forward. I catch a glimpse of something moving towards the train off to my right. With my eyes still adjusting to the dark, I can't tell if I'm seeing things or if there's an actual figure alongside the track. My head jerks backwards slightly as my car is the last part of the train to begin its steady climb up a hill. The outlines of multiple figures can now be seen moving towards me. Their out stretched arms appearing out of the darkness reaching towards me. The train with its' continued clacking pulling me up and away from their presence. I feel like I'm just safely out of their reach when a clawed hand appears and scratches my cheek. I turn sideways afraid for fear of a continued attack, but behind me I see only black. I sit back completely in my seat and secure myself again wondering what could possibly come next. Suddenly the noise stops and the train accelerates over the last few feet of an incline. Then my stomach pulls up in my chest as we begin to plummet down a very steep hill. I hear screams but I can't tell if they're coming from the other passengers or something else.

We roar through the bottom of the hill and I'm lifted briefly off my seat as we speed over another smaller hill. As the train dips down again before shooting back up over yet another hill, I see more figures near to the side of the tracks. My grip tightens. They seem to be making a high pitched screeching sound that makes the hairs stand up straight on my arms and neck. It's almost as if they're crying out at being denied the opportunity to get a hold of myself and the other riders. Instead, we zip by out of reach and into a few more hairpin twists and turns. I wonder how long my strength will keep if I have to continue to hold on as tightly as I am. Any more wicked turns and my neck might surely break.

The train races into a sharp turn upwards and we are suddenly above ground again. It's nighttime and we're traveling on an elevated rail system. I have a view of a metropolitan skyline with a cluster of residential apartment buildings nearby. A single silhouette stands out in the distance that I recognize as what was once called the Sears tower. The city is dark not just because it's night, but because there is no power anywhere. Scattered fires in several buildings and throughout the streets are the only light. Distant screams and gun fire fill my ears. Clearly some sort of natural disaster or man-made catastrophe has brought this city to its knees. It makes me wonder what would be better; the horror filled ride I've been traveling on or the apocalyptic scene beside me? As if the decision is taken out of my hands, the train drops suddenly back underground and into darkness.

A few more zigzag turns and speeding towards a set of monstrous doors that continue to open and close like elevator doors. The doors look to be made up of large links from a metal chain, with each link being larger than a school bus and as the doors slam closed the earth shakes. I can read the timing of the opening and closing of the doors to realize that they will slam shut next just as the train would be passing through it. It looks as though we're about to be crushed. As the train reaches the threshold I close my eyes anticipating the impending crunch. A loud crash happens and I open my eyes to see that we've made it through safely. My body relaxes with relief, but I know it's only momentary. On the opposite side I see our tracks lead into a tiny crevice on the rock wall in front of us. We speed through the opening and I have to duck my head to avoid having it ripped from my body. And then again, into the darkness.

The train which had been slowing suddenly jerks forward as an unseen chain again connects with the underside and slowly begins to pull it up yet another steep hill. The darkness is filled with the clicking from the train as it is being pulled ever upwards. My ears begin to hurt from the loud pounding of the repetitive noise. Just when I feel that my head can take no more, the sound stops. We've reached the crest and I prepare myself for another

133

dive. The train not only drops this time, but drops with no tracks beneath it into complete blackness. My stomach free falls along with the plummet. Somewhere in the back of my mind I realize that this is the point in all dreams where you wake up suddenly. That supposedly if you don't wake up and actually hit the ground from falling in your dream, you will die in real life. Suddenly, light appears beneath me as the ground can be seen rushing up to meet the falling train.

Below us in another massive cavern more creatures like before, can now be seen everywhere. Thousands of them! Demons anxiously waiting for the train full of passengers to hit the ground so that they can finally get their fangs and claws into us. I understand now that this is our final destination. Where we would spend the rest of eternity being torn apart, piece by piece, with each tear being more painful than the last. I wonder what it was that I did in my life to deserve to end up here. What possibly could have been the deciding factor that I deserved this fate? I feel like I had lived a good life. Treating others as you would treat yourself was what we were supposed to do, right? We all make mistakes and were mine truly that bad? Or is it simply that we ALL end up here? Punishment for having just lived life, regardless of how we lived it. My heart breaks with the feeling of having been cheated. Like having studied years for a final exam only to find out just before the test that you'd been given the wrong textbook.

Out of the corner of my eye I see a small glimmer of hope that the train may actually survive the fall and with it the possibility that I might make it thru beyond this hell. Below us, beside a river of lava are more tracks. Except with the speed of the free fall and the angle of the train I can quickly tell that the cars will not land on the tracks. Instead we crash into the ground near the tracks where I immediately feel a wave of hot water blast into my ear and over the side of my face.

The noise and the force of the water are finally enough to wake me from this horror filled nightmare. I am awake and in my bed with my heart racing. So real was the blast that I thought for sure as I awoke that I would be drenched. Surprisingly, my pillow and sheets are dry. The unnerving dream continues to rebound through my head trying to break through the barrier of my slumber. My body feeling like it has been beaten up and my mind questioning what was really real.

I climb out of my bed trying to get as far away from the space where these images had come to me. Thinking a splash of fresh water would help clear them from my head, I move towards the bathroom on unstable legs. As the lights come on my eyes burn from the brightness. I painfully force my eye lids open wishing desperately for them to adjust faster to the glare. I turn on the faucets and fill my hands with cold water. I quickly bring my hands up to my face and repeat this action in a vain attempt to wash away the recent visions. But the comfort of this material world is only brief as there, reflected back to me in the mirror, is something that had not there the night before. My fingers reach up to my face as if in disbelief. A long scratch mark with fresh blood shines bright on my cheek, with a stinging that screams that this was no dream.

CARVED IN STONE

By Frank Roger

Prologue

The letters danced before Brother Magnus's eyes and he had to stop writing for a few moments. He had been working for too long and couldn't keep up his concentration. After a while his vision cleared and he reread the last few paragraphs he had copied. Something didn't appear quite correct and he checked it against the original text.

My God, he thought. I've made a few mistakes. It must have been the fatigue, along with the tedium of the work in the scriptorium. So what do I do now? There's no way to correct the errors, not on the precious and delicate material they used here in the monastery. Too bad cheap paper was a thing of the past... like so many other things.

He thought and shook his head. Did those few mistakes really matter? Who would discover them? Who would compare his copy with the original text? And if someone did, how could he possibly find out which scribe was responsible for these blunders? Magnus was convinced he needn't worry.

He looked at the other scribes who were hard at work, and wondered what went on in their minds. Did they always take their sacred mission seriously?

He took a deep breath and resumed his work. Damned, he thought, as he realised he had made another mistake. I should be more careful. He reread the accidentally altered passage and had to repress a chuckle. The idea that he had changed a line of the Holy Scriptures filled him with joy, whereas he ought to have felt deep shame.

He went on copying, deliberately making more mistakes, as he found this practice provided him with some welcome relief from the unending boredom of a scribe's task. As a matter of fact, it was more than mere relief. What he felt was pleasure.

He kept writing and diverging from the original text, his mood brightening.

Chapter 1. The Seed

"Brother Magnus."

The Abbot shot him a cold, hard stare. Brother Magnus understood bad news was coming. The Abbot never requested to see one of the Brothers to break him good news. And Magnus had little doubt as to the subject of his superior's displeasure.

"It would appear you put in a fair amount of work in the scriptorium lately, which speaks indisputably in your favour. However, it has come to my attention that the quality of the work you deliver is not quite proportionate to the number of hours you spend there. Brother Magnus, let us recapitulate the basics of a scribe's mission."

The Abbot leaned back in his seat, his gaze penetrating deep into Magnus's eyes. The flickering light of the candles on his desk lent his face an ominous quality. Magnus wished the candles would not only give light, but also warmth. It was cold in here, as in the entire monastery, with the exception of the scriptorium – now the Abbot was not supposed to find out that for some that was a valid reason for spending so much time there.

"What is a scribe's task, Brother Magnus, and what higher purpose does it serve?"

Magnus swallowed and said:

"We copy the Holy Scriptures. As the number of copies of the Holy Scriptures increases, the sacred wisdom will be distributed more widely and bring enlightenment to more people who are now groping in the dark."

"That is quite correct. Now, what is the main rule of conduct for a scribe?"

"To remain faithful to the words of the Holy Scriptures."

"Meaning that…"

"The words of the Holy Scriptures are as if carved in stone. Changing even one letter is heresy."

"Very well, Brother Magnus. It would appear you have a sound understanding of the theory. Now, as to the way this theory is put into practice…"

The Abbot did not finish his sentence. He took the manuscript on his desk, and turned a few pages. Magnus cringed as he saw it was his work. Had the Abbot suspected anything? Or did he actually read and check all the copies made in the Scriptorium? Or had he simply stumbled upon his latest effort and accidentally spotted something that sparked his wrath?

"I have gone over this manuscript, and to my horror I noticed it was different from the text of the Holy Scriptures. At first it was just a couple of words, which might be due to a few moments of inattention by a tired scribe. However, as I continued to read, the text turned out to deviate more and more from the original. I had the feeling I was being presented with an alternative version of the Holy Scriptures. How would we call this, Brother Magnus?"

"Heresy," he replied.

"Quite correct, Brother. Now, I believe this manuscript is your work?"

"It is indeed."

The Abbot paused for dramatic effect. His piercing stare almost hurt Magnus's eyes.

"Brother Magnus, I believe I'm entitled to a few words of explanation."

Now what do I tell him? Brother Magnus thought. There were two possibilities. Either he told the Abbot the truth, that he was growing increasingly disenchanted with the tedium of life in the monastery, with the Abbot's unfailing support of the religious authorities, with the prospect of a life serving ideals he was no longer fully behind. That he enjoyed working in the scriptorium mainly because it was the only heated part of the monastery (the only way to keep the ink sufficiently liquid) and that the changes he had introduced in the text were the products of a mind eager to break free from routine and add a few moments of joy to what would otherwise be a mind-numbing endeavour. It was true that he had derived great pleasure from these bouts of creative writing.

Or he could tell him that he had consciously deviated from the Holy Scriptures, wishing to present his personal version of the text that stuck closer to his unorthodox ideals and his dreams of a better world, liberated from the yoke of the religious hardliners.

The first explanation would result in forced physical labour for the rest of his days, without any hope of redemption or any chance at leaving the confines of the monastery.

The second explanation would lead to excommunication: he would be thrown out of the monastery, dropped into the harsh reality beyond its safe walls, left to his own devices without any support from his religious community.

It was not a difficult choice.

"Brother Magnus," the Abbot said. "I asked you a question. Are you still pondering your reply? How do you explain the mistakes you made?"

He looked the Abbot straight into the eyes and said: "They are not mistakes."

The Abbot's cold gaze transfixed him. He felt as if the temperature in the room had suddenly dropped a few degrees.

"I found the Holy Scriptures no longer matched my personal views, and chose to adapt them accordingly."

For a few moments there was silence. Total and utter silence.

When the Abbot spoke again, his voice was reduced to a whisper, as if he dared not speak aloud.

"Brother Magnus, do you realise what you are saying?"

"Yes, I do," he replied.

"Do you know how this kind of erring is called?"

"Yes. It is called heresy."

"And do you know what fate is reserved for a heretic?"

"Yes," he answered. "I know it very well."

Chapter 2. The Dawn

Magnus realised he should be thankful for the cold. Without the harsh winter temperature he might not have taken refuge in the tavern, and would probably have missed out on the opportunity of his life. And former monks were not usually offered too many opportunities.

He had been unceremoniously kicked out of the monastery, clutching his few possessions, without a clue as to what his next move would be. He had made it to the nearby town of Hogg's Moor, shivering in his tunic that was way too light for this time of year.

The tavern on the market square had attracted him like a magnet, even if he feared he would not be allowed in, as he did have no money to spend. Chilled to the bone as he was, he decided to take the risk and went in.

To his relief no one asked him any questions. Maybe it was because the tavern was packed with people, talking and drinking and eating, that his presence went unnoticed.

He was pondering his options as he discovered he was not the only person here without money to spend.

At one point a man climbed upon a table and performed a juggling act with balls and other objects. Most people hardly paid attention to him, but some watched and applauded, and threw him a handful of coins. Sometime later, in the opposite corner, another man presented an act of comedy, eliciting both catcalls and laughter. While some people booed him off the table, others rewarded him with some money. Shortly thereafter Magnus noticed the man had ordered a simple meal and a pint of beer. Had he really made that much?

So it was possible for people with a particular talent to get by here, even if only in a very modest way. But how could a former monk work his way into this system? He could not sing or play an instrument, perform tricks or present any kind of show. He was just a heretic without any redeeming qualities.

Unless he somehow managed to transform his heresy into an act that might interest these tavern folk enough to favour him with some money. But how could he do that? He was about to discard the very idea as ludicrous, when hunger and thirst convinced him to give it a try anyhow. It was clear this would be his only short term chance to make a living, the only alternative being life as a mendicant, a bleak prospect considering the total lack of respect for excommunicated monks.

But what could he do then? What could he tell these people, how could he grab their attention and win them over, so as to make them part with some of their hard-earned money?

If I just sit here considering my next move I may well starve to death before I come up with anything, he realised. I'd better get up on a table and improvise. We'll see if I get away with it.

So he gathered his courage, climbed upon a table and said in a voice loud enough to drown the din:

"I've seen the light. And I can make you see the light as well."

A few heads turned into his direction, but most people ignored him, happy to empty their pints, eat their food and talk to their table companions.

He kept talking about his "vision," and gradually his speech degraded into a diatribe against the ruling religious authorities, and ended with a call for support for his "march towards enlightenment and a better world. Let me to show you the way. Embrace freedom, throw off the smothering yoke of the ruling priesthood. Let their monasteries crumble to debris."

Then he stood panting with the exertion, hoping for some reaction, but all he got was a sneer:

"We've seen better comic relief here."

He came back down from his table, sorely disappointed. He had reached hardly anyone, and had not even collected one single coin. So he would starve to death here anyhow. Clearly his "act" was not what these tavern folk were used to.

He was about to give in to despair as a man and a woman approached him.

"We need to talk," the man said. "But not in here. The wrong ears might hear us."

"You should eat something first," the woman added. "You look as if you could use it. And you need warm clothes. These flimsy garments of yours are worthless. Let us take care of all that."

"Who are you?" he asked. "What is all this about?"

"We represent a small underground organisation. Your little speech there struck a chord with us. Your ideas happen to be very close to what we're fighting for. But in order to succeed, we need a focus, a flag carrier, someone we can rally behind. It might be you."

"I'm a heretic," he said. "A monk excommunicated for his ideas." He thought it wise not to expand too much on the reasons for his dismissal.

"No, you're not a heretic. You're a prophet."

"Our prophet," the woman confirmed. "We need one."

That's it, he thought. My first disciples. I thought I didn't make an impression, but instead found what might be the vanguard of an army eager to overthrow the ruling priesthood. Of course he had no idea that his vision was shared by even a small number of dissidents.

"Please follow us," the man said, grabbing his arm.

"All right," he replied, knowing very well that his options were limited. For now he enjoyed the prospect of a hot meal and warm clothes. The rest could wait.

Chapter 3. The Rise

"I've seen the light," Magnus bellowed out. "And I can make you see the light as well."

His preaches had become a routine he delivered passionately and convincingly. The fact that his small band of disciples kept any trouble-shooters or disgruntled supporters of the ruling class at bay worked wonders for his confidence. It was a good thing he was surrounded by faithful followers, armed and ready to stand their ground. In some towns they had been chased away, and his faithful crew had to keep him out of harm's way. After all he was not exactly preaching to the converted.

This time he was fairly lucky. He was able to perform his entire "speech" without being interrupted, without facing any hostility from the religious authorities.

Now this didn't necessarily mean that his audience was a receptive one, even if he had honed his "act" to perfection by now, travelling from village to village in the hope to win over as many as possible for his cause.

When he had finished, Magnus and his group retreated to the outskirts of town, where they ate and drank a little. Four men approached them, and his disciples immediately took their positions. They needn't have worried: the newcomers asked if they could join them. They had seen the light and wanted to be part of Magnus's rising movement. He welcomed them and thanked them for their support.

It was clear to Magnus that he was on the right track. The very fact that he often ran into trouble with representatives of the religious authorities meant that they already considered him a serious competitor. But with each town he visited, his army of followers grew and would soon be a force to be reckoned with.

Later that night, as he was about to retire to his tent, two persons were waiting for him in the gathering twilight. They were the man and the woman who had become his first disciples, back when he had faced despair in Hogg's Moor's tavern.

"Brother Magnus," the man called Glen said. "There is something we would like to discuss. Do you have a few moments for us?"

"Certainly. Is there a problem? Something you are unhappy with?"

They shook their heads. "No. Our movement is growing, and one day soon we will realise our goal. It's just that something is missing."

"Your preaching is eloquent and efficient," the woman, called Gwenny, said, "but it is just spoken words. A movement like ours should have more than that."

"Are you saying we need our own Holy Scriptures?"

"Yes, Brother Magnus. We need our own Holy Scriptures. We need a text to learn and recite, we need a book to brandish as we defend our faith. It is more than a symbol. It's a basis, a foundation to build on."

Magnus nodded appreciatively. "An excellent suggestion. I will give it serious thought."

The couple wished him good night and disappeared. Magnus retired into his tent and considered the idea of writing his own Holy Scriptures. The prospect appealed to him. It would take a lot of time and energy, and it would be hard to pull off as he crisscrossed the land with his army of disciples. The ideal thing would be to build a monastery, with a scriptorium where the work might be done in good conditions. The monastery might also serve as his power base, the center from which his influence would spread.

He could not see how he might go about it in the near future, but in the longer term it was definitely an option with considerable merit.

Would his own Holy Scriptures, a sacred text based solely on his views, one day rival the existing ones, perhaps even drive them out completely? The idea pleased him. He would definitely try to turn it into a reality.

His own monastery, his own Holy Scriptures… He would have plenty to dream about that night.

Chapter 4. Consolidation

"Hail the Prophet! Hail the Prophet!"

Magnus strode out into the early morning light and greeted the cheering crowd waiting for him in front of the monastery's massive entrance. He spread his arms wide and said:

"I've seen the light."

"We've seen the light too," the crowd chanted in perfect unison.

"This is a day of celebration," he cried out.

"We'll celebrate," his followers roared.

We have a lot to celebrate indeed, he thought, as he slowly made his way through the throng towards Hogg's Moor's market square. This village, where he had started his campaign for a better world, was the first one to have fallen for his message. There were hardly any partisans of the "old church" left, and its monastery was slowly crumbling to dust. Other villages would undoubtedly follow, and soon Magnus's movement would be the prime religious force in the region.

There was just no stopping it; it was a tidal wave washing away all that it found in its path.

His very own Holy Scriptures were being copied in his scriptorium by a staff of devoted scribes, and a second and a third monastery were being built. There was reason for celebration indeed.

But first there was urgent business to attend to in the market square. A speech, and this time he would be preaching to the converted. And the Burning, for which no doubt a fair crowd would show up. After all it was the first one ever.

Magnus quickened his pace, and his disciples followed him, cheering and chanting passages from the Scriptures. He felt elated as he reached the market square, climbed onto the stage that was prepared for him and let his gaze roam in all directions.

The market square was crammed full with people, and to his right he could see the tavern where his adventure had begun, years ago, when he was just an excommunicated monk.

He waited for the crowd to turn silent and delivered his speech, glorifying his achievements and reveling in the downfall of the old church. He interspersed his words with the slogans that had become his hallmark, to which the faithful chanted the replies:

"I've seen the light."

"We've seen the light too."

"A better world is beckoning."

"The Prophet will lead us."

He made a sweeping gesture that encompassed both the market square and the sky, and thousands of throats yelled:

"Hail the Prophet! Hail the Prophet!"

When the formal part of the speech was done, he drew the crowd's attention to the two funeral pyres at his left.

"The time has now come for a momentous occasion."

"The Burning," they chanted, "the Burning."

"Who wrote the Holy Scriptures?"

"The Prophet! The Prophet!"

"Let it be known that the words of the Holy Scriptures are as if carved in stone. Not one word may be changed! Not one single word!"

"Hail the Prophet!" they shouted. "Hail the Prophet!" His disciples were growing excited; he could feel their fervor rising, almost tangible in the air. It was clear they were ready for what was to come.

"What is the just punishment for those who dare to deviate from the Scriptures?" he asked.

"The Burning! The Burning!"

"Proceed," he ordered his men.

Soon the two men on their funeral pyres were engulfed by flames, and the acrid smell of burning flesh struck his nostrils. The gathered believers went completely mad, as if the death of the two heretics also washed away all their collective sins.

Magnus watched the spectacle approvingly. The two heretics had been loyal followers of his, until recently. They had been employed in his scriptorium, making copies of his Holy Scriptures, which were highly in demand as the success of his religion rose.

He had discovered the errors in their texts by chance. He didn't know if these two scribes had knowingly made alterations to his Holy Scriptures. Maybe they had merely been tired and made some mistakes while copying. But actually that didn't matter. What mattered was that they had deviated from his holy text, had changed words that were as if carved in stone.

And he couldn't tolerate that. He just could not take the risk. He knew all too well where this might lead to.

GOOD DOG

By Chris Moylan

A dog is a dog. Food for dogs is good for dogs. Food for dogs is good and it is for dogs; it is good for dogs. The scent leads to the prey, the prey is food for dogs. Food for dogs is good for dogs. The scent is good, the prey is good. For dogs.

That is the logic of dogs. That is the way of dogs. We run and sleep. We read the scents and from time to time we hunt. We read the scents because we are dogs and dogs read the scents. We follow the scents where they lead and we read them scrupulously, with absolute attention. Because we are dogs and dogs read the scents. We run when the prey runs or flies. We catch the prey when we can and sink our teeth into the sweet flesh. Then we sleep. This is what we do. We are dogs.

Dogs that are not dogs do not read the scents, do not shove their snouts into the grass and dig for the source of the scent down to the rich dirt written over with scents: blood, urine, food, bone and turd. Nor do they dig beneath the surface of the dirt for the source and, from time to time, the prey. Conversely, we do not stand over the dogs that are not dogs and wait for the snuffling of the scent or the shoving of the snout in the dirt. We do not command that it be so. Dogs that are not dogs are not dogs. It would be absurd to stand on our back legs like they do and bark "Dig! Dig!" so that the reading of the scent commence and all attention narrow to the richness of what has been deposited or sprinkled or liberally sprayed or left inadvertently, or indifferently, as a trace on the rich dirt. Nothing useful would occur.

Dogs that are not dogs are not dogs. The ratio of scent to time to distance is invisible and unknown to them. The grammar of stink is lost to them; they cannot read it or trace its history in the wind or on the earth. The stink circulates around them and they do not feel its caress. It drapes on their fur and they do not hear it or feel it. It calls to them and they do not hear it. One wonders how they manage to breed or feed themselves.

And yet. And yet there was a time when dogs that are not dogs controlled the hunt, blind as they were. They required that dogs that are dogs begin the hunt and stop the hunt. Begin the reading of the scent and stop the reading of the scent. Stop mid-scent and stay while the scent went on speaking this way and that way, drifting down into the earth and in mounds upon the earth, flowing in the breeze and in the water that ran along the earth, so much to read and follow, this way and that way. Stay. Stay!

Good dog. The dogs who are not dogs followed the dogs that are dogs in the reading of the scent.

Then "stay!" Dogs stayed and dogs that are not dogs stayed. The prey flew for a short distance and dropped, as birds do. We ran to the prey and took it in our teeth, prepared to shake the prey, break its neck and sink our teeth into the sweet flesh. But the prey was wood, or some other thing that is not prey. The dogs that are not dogs commanded that the prey that is not prey be brought to them and deposited on the rich earth for them to take. And the dogs that are not dogs took the prey that is not prey and made it fly again. They ordered the dogs that are dogs to hunt, seize the prey that was not prey and return the prey that was not prey to the dog that was not a dog. This was not what a dog does. Yet the dog did what it was commanded to do; pain is not good for dogs. All this became what a dog does.

"Good dog."

The dog that did these things was a good dog. But what is that? A dog is a dog. Not a good dog. Food for dogs is good for dogs. Sleep for dogs is good for dogs. But dogs are not good. Dogs

150

are dogs. A dog is not good for the hunt, the sprinkle of urine, the sleep after eating. A dog is a dog. Such is the way of dogs, such is the logic of dogs.

What was a good dog for? A good dog is good for dogs that are not dogs. Therefore, a good dog was not a dog...Yet it was a dog. This was impossible, yet it was. Thus the change. Commands for dogs were good for dogs. Fetch. Stay. Paw. Good. Good dog was good for dogs. Good was good for dogs. Good dog.

But good, what was that? Good had no scent or trail, no neck or sweet flesh to tear and eat. And yet. Good was the command. The command was good. Good for dogs.

The scent remained and the reading of the scent. The prey remained, sitting by the front gate, for example, plump and fresh with meat, its eye fixed on the dog straining to seize the neck and pierce the sweet flesh. But the command was "stay." We ran to seize the prey and the result was pain. Bad dog.

Bad was bad for dogs. Bad dog was pain was bad for dogs. Bad dog was bad for dogs.

The dogs were not masters of consistency, or of logic for that matter. They persisted in leaping, straining, and running towards the cat, rabbit or squirrel. But the masters were masters of consistency, and pain. They were impervious to high stench or new urine. They turned their noses from anal suasion, the most ancient and honored of rhetoric. And yet. They controlled food for dogs. Good dogs ate the food for dogs. Following the commands made bad dogs good and good dogs good, snouts in the meat. Good was good for dogs. Good was good.

Good was in the air, scent like, more powerful than a call or whine. Good was near and sharp, good was hard as wood. It could not be bitten or torn apart. It would not suffer its neck to be broken, or for it to lie limp and yielding, eyes blank with acceptance. Only paw, stay, go, sit, roll over, good boy gave good, made good.

One day a dog, a good dog, jumped when commanded to jump and, in jumping, became a good jumping dog. He became the good of jumping. Stop could not penetrate this perfection. "Down!" failed to convert him. How could it? Down is merely the reversal of jump, the absence of the force that propels a dog into the air, the force of good. Other dogs on their walks saw this demonstration of good, and jumped in response. And jumped. And jumped. Other dogs that were dogs within sight or hearing of these dogs jumped as well. The command to "stop!" trailed after them, a wounded prey, and its force dripping in doubt on the hard ground.

Dogs that are dogs beyond counting jumped beyond counting. They ignored the food and water that was presented to them and jumped away from the pain-dealing sticks and paws that lashed at them. The command that is good, the good that is command were joined as the teeth are joined to the snout. Outside these was nothing; the dogs that were not dogs stopped their stumbling on two paws, no longer mated or pushed the food into their snouts with sticks and other things. The jumping was everywhere: in the dens and outside the dens, in the fields and in the paths of death-dealing things the dogs that were not dogs moved on the hard ground. Dark followed light and light dark and still the dogs jumped, following the command.

"Bad dog! Bad dog!" The bad that is good pulled the dogs up, and the good that is bad pulled them higher and the good that is good had little of the stink of good bad, bad good, none of its piney sting and old flesh musk, none of its high humming rot. Jumping, countless dogs sank their teeth in the neck of good and broke its neck, and falling sank their teeth in the good, and broke its neck, tearing the rich flesh to drink of nothingness where the moon opens its bloom and all the stinks of the world cry out. On the third day, all of the dogs beyond counting dropped to the hard ground and fell asleep.

I turned the corner onto the side street near my house in Queens. It was a warm spring morning, humid and vaguely sunny through the haze. Weeks of alternating rain and warmth made for a weird brilliance in the cherry blossoms. Pollen dusted the windows of parked cars and the filaments of linden blossoms coated the sidewalks. A street cleaner, portly and graceful, rolled down the block with a pleasant shush-shush sound from its rotating brushes and twirled around to make a wider pass. A young mother pushed her baby carriage down the block while behind her an elderly widow shoved her shopping cart forward inch by inch, an old man closing in on both, shoulders rounded and large hands dangling as if he couldn't decide whether to grab one broad bottom or push the other into oncoming traffic.

A dog floated by. Then another. A peripheral bounce of legs and fur dropped at eye level and disappeared, rose to eye level again. A black poodle, a golden lab, a Chihuahua, another golden lab. A stream of dogs, dozens in synchronized run jump run movements flowing in parabolic waves from east to west down the block.

The old man sank down on his haunches, arms dropping to his sides, and watched the dogs parade by. The mother lifted her child from the carriage and ran up a flight of brick steps to a courtyard garden. The carriage rolled into the street and was hit by a car, exploding in a panic of baby toys and pink blankets and swerving cars. Drivers jumped out to see who or what had been hit and were knocked over by dogs. Dogs ran straight down the middle of the avenue, joined by a constant stream of other dogs from every direction, some dragging leashes, some with their halters torn. My own dog, a middle aged Shih Tzu mix ordinarily no more active than a bag of socks, leaped from the wall in the front yard and scampered down the street after the rest, and a contract between us was irreparably broken.

Traffic stopped on Northern and the side streets with dogs weaving through the lanes, leaping in front of startled drivers, slamming into cars when the crush of other dogs cut them mid-leap, their black nails scoring the hoods as they came down. Several drivers leaned on their horns, and the sound was answered throughout western Queens, first a few cars then dozens and quickly hundreds, an aggregate static moan rolling out towards the East River like a cloud of dust.

Through the noise I saw a pantomime of attempts to bring the dogs back: some slapping their thighs and calling, some waving, others cupping hands to their mouths and dipping at the knees to put all their strength into a call few could hear over the car horns and screams and calls. A good many people decided that the dogs were just first warning sign of an impending natural catastrophe. An earthquake. A tidal wave. A sun flare. The instinct was to run for shelter in a basement or an open space. But a place that made sense for an earthquake didn't make sense for a tidal wave, and nothing made sense for an alien invasion, which quickly became the most widely held theory. For those unconvinced by any of those possibilities the only recourse was to run like hell or sag to the sidewalk and weep. And what if one person wanted to run and another to stay? I saw a man pulling a woman by the hair toward a row house, a woman slap her child in the face and drag him by the arm towards an apartment building. Lovers screamed at each other and turned on anyone foolish enough to intervene, kicking and punching the would-be Good Samaritan into a pulp.

We ran away from the mayhem and after our dogs, we the masters, the owners, in our bare feet and running shoes, workout clothes and business suits, mostly late middle aged men and women chasing the soft bulbs of our bellies wobbling vaguely

154

toward the dogs, the weak stems of our arms rowing and pumping after a gazelle-like tide of four legged athletes racing through the neighborhood. When we lost sight of the dogs we set course by the swarm of helicopters chuffing over and around the Queensborough Bridge. When our breath gave out, we pulled hipsters off their slick ultra-light ten-speed bicycles and gave chase again. When people got in our way, we kicked them aside, hard. They got angry and we turned back and kicked them in the face. Fuck them.

Traffic everywhere had stalled, with a chaos of dogs rushing from all directions to join the main group. Dogs caught indoors howled to get out, dogs on walks strained to pull free from their owners. And all this running, jumping, barking of dogs set something free in people nearby. Groups of teenage boys ran through stalled cars, moving with that run-skip of kids beside themselves with excitement. Police cruisers whooped-whooped to get through traffic. Store owners chambered bullets in their rifles and stood outside their front doors. Drinkers and the late lunch crowd at The Boil and Bubble wandered into the street, beer mugs in hand, and tried with no success to kick and trip the dogs as they ran past.

I didn't notice much of this; I was pedaling as hard as I could and trying not to hit anything that skittered past me. I was tiring, not so much from the exertion of pedaling as from the assault of car horns, screams and laughter, and dog cries of every timbre and description. By the time we reached the Queensborough Bridge a half dozen cars were burning on the Queens bound outer ramp. Dogs flowed through the flames and past the flames, an endless tide of dogs joined by a growing tide of people abandoning their cars and running after them.

For days we tracked the dogs. Our original group of half a dozen was joined by others along the way; by the time we left the Bronx there were about two dozen of us: all male, most young guys in slick biking suits and helmets, fit and lean. We slept only a few hours each night and took our meals where we could find them. We rummaged through trashed food carts and delivery trucks, burnt out grocery stores. We even picked through cars abandoned in the early panic. One of our crew happened upon a car just as a looting party arrived; he took a bullet in the face. Another was pulled from his bike and stabbed; when I looked back at him he was kneeling in the street, his arm around his open gut. The rest of us learned our lesson after that and rode with metal pipes and other improvised weapons grabbed along the way.

The crowds thinned as we pedaled north of the city into Westchester. We didn't know what was happening behind us. After only a week the smoke to the south blocked our view of the city, and it was no longer unusual to encounter bodies along the road. By the time we reached the rural areas of Putnam County the roads were entirely deserted. Even the helicopters that had been trailing the dogs were gone.

I don't know why we kept going. We missed our dogs, of course, and hoped that by some odd chance we might be reunited with them. More than that, we wanted to understand what had happened. Why had all those dogs behaved that way? Was it a virus? A response, as some among us believed, to a Pentagon signaling program gone bad? If it was a panic behavior in anticipation of an impending catastrophe, why that behavior and why all dogs?

We rested finally, taking shelter in a strip mall supermarket just outside Cold Spring. Everything of value there had been ransacked but we found a Chinese takeout nearby with a rice cooker still full and a rack of spear ribs in the broiler, plus a bottle of single malt whiskey that had rolled under a counter in the liquor store. Everything else was either stolen or smashed.

Including the windows and neon signs. It was while we were sleeping off the ribs and whiskey that the dogs came.

I woke, as I had so many times in my life, to a tongue in my ear. A dog was working away, assiduously licking ear, neck, and brow. I must been layered in salt from riding for so long, a lovely dirty mess for a dog. I pushed him away, my eyes closed. I could not trust the one in a million chance that it could be my dog. But I had to open my eyes eventually, and there he was, Tinker, cleaning me as if we were back in Queens waking to just another sunny day. He was noticeably thinner and his fur had knotted and matted to the consistency of a plush rug left in the rain. He shied from my hand when I reached to pat him and lowered his head in the attack position. My heart broke.

I scraped together a carton of rice and scraps of meat and gristle from the discarded ribs and pushed it towards him across the floor. He took the carton in his teeth and ran past the automatic door. I followed him, padding awkwardly on bare feet. The other riders were gone. The bikes were where we left them the night before, and the rolled up coats and shirts the riders used for blankets were scattered around the store as if everyone had gone out to answer a call of nature.

It was just dawn. Outside, dogs beyond counting filled the parking lot and hill behind it, and every road, lot, sidewalk, and park in sight. Tinker dropped the carton in a mountainous pile of other food scraps to the left of the supermarket and trotted into the pack. Beside the food were bowls of water, hundreds of them left in a parking lot. Several other mounds of food rose before buildings across the length of the small town. I waited for the dogs to move, and they studied me, as dogs do.

While I was watching the dogs people emerged from the buildings nearby. They walked slowly, some from fear, many from the effects of illness or loss of blood. Clusters of children walked up from hiding places by the river. Groups of women moved in proximity but never mingling with the kids, never getting too close. They formed rows on either side of the mound of food and back toward the hills overlooking the town. They were tired and confused. Some were barely able to stand but they waited, not moving, while the last stragglers joined them. The dogs, for their part, sat like little Buddhas, watching. Every now and then a formation, as I thought of them, peeled off to pee by the river, trotting back in the same geometric arrangement as if under command to do so.

After an hour all everyone was in place, a couple of thousand humans facing many thousands of dogs, separated by a space of about fifty yards, a zone that not even the children cared to enter. At once, the dogs stood up on their hind legs, held position, dropped to a sitting position, extended right paw, then left paw. They barked, then barked again, the noise so loud it shook the ground. In a moment, the ground shook again as deer, thousands of them, came down from the hills and stood at the fringe of trees, grinning, white tails showing, necks straining forward, eyes wide open and intent. Looking at us.

The dogs rolled over and played dead. They held out the left paw, then the right, and sat up begging with both paws held chest high. They jumped, then crawled bellies low to the ground. Then they advanced, jumping as they had weeks before, barking and growling, advancing towards us slowly, teeth bare. Demanding a response before the last leap.

THE LOVED BOY

By Jill Boyles

Broken pieces settled in his heels and slept until his father died. When awakened, they traveled up his body to his mind, lodging in his lower consciousness under the veneer of knowing, where in his dreams he heard a mother hen squawk. In the mornings, he rubbed sand from his eyes that also cleared away any lingering squawks. It was as though he were taking care of the business of life he couldn't attend to in the real world that felt nebulous as if he were somewhere outside of it, suspended somewhere in the sky, watching himself move through the days and nights. Sometimes, he reached out an arm, and with a finger, nudged the bubble of his existence.

The Hotel Restaurant

The waiter's arm shook as he put a plate of asparagus with hollandaise sauce between the prostitute and him.

"Will there be anything else for the lovely couple?" the waiter asked.

"No," he replied.

"Very good, Sir. Enjoy."

He looked up into the waiter's sallow skin and saw regrets clattering down his wrinkles like rain jittering down a rusted, corrugated roof. As the waiter shuffled away, he imagined those regrets spooling off him and onto the floor, skulking toward his own shoes. He lifted his feet onto the claw leg of the table.

"I feel bad for not helping that old waiter." She picked up the plate and set it back down. "Heavy."

"He's capable of doing his job."

"The world'd be better if we all helped each other." She tipped the sauce boat over the asparagus. The air wafted butter, lemon and egg yolk.

"How do you propose I help you?"

She brought an entire spear dripping of sauce to her lips and winked.

He swallowed his Scotch. He should have chosen the other girl, the taller one, who had a modicum of elegance, but she suffered a dearth of tits.

She picked up her glass and sniffed and swirled the wine.

"A wine enthusiast?"

"Sort of." She took a sip and another and then a longer one. After putting the glass down, she dunked a finger in the sauce boat, slid it into her mouth and extracted it slowly.

He leaned over the table. "Do you mind?"

"What?" She rubbed her nyloned toes against his inner thigh.

"Not here." He scanned the restaurant's dim interior to see if anyone had noticed, but as far as he could tell no one had. Among the patrons, he spotted two prostitutes and four escorts – one he had used before. Next time, he would be less parsimonious and pay for that escort again, yet when it came down to it, a hole was a hole.

The prostitute severed another spear with her teeth. A bead of sauce like a yellow malignant beauty mark hung just below her lower lip and moved up and down as she chewed. Her throaty approvals sounded like groans of ecstasy reaching out to throttle him.

From the gloom of an impassive sky, he watched himself through the skylight in the restaurant's roof. Watched himself in that bubble. Watched himself lift water to his lips. Watched himself take in the water and try to swallow. His mouth turned into a sea. The prostitute jammed the rest of the spear into her mouth; up and down, up and down bobbed the yellow mole, the throaty throttle, he couldn't swallow so clamped his lips shut to keep the sea from surging down his chin and onto his shirt and pants.

"A penny for your thoughts."

The caesura startled him, and he almost lost the sea. He put his hand over his mouth. Open your goddamn throat and swallow. Open the floodgates, open sesame, open that pipe, but the sea crashed against the dike every time.

"Here it coooomes." The prostitute clapped.

He pursed his lips tighter at her condescending comment, thinking it was directed toward him. Yet, when he looked at her, she was looking elsewhere. He followed her gaze to the waiter balancing two plates of food.

He dipped his chin and swooped it outward like a cartoon character swallowing gum and drained the sea.

"Herb roasted chicken for the lady." The waiter put the plate in front of the prostitute.

"And, for the gentleman, rare, dry aged sirloin steak." The plate wobbled in front of him. "Will there be anything else for the lovely couple?"

"No." He coughed.

"Pardon?"

"No."

"Very good, Sir. Enjoy."

He cut a large piece of steak and studied the cross-section of the animal's erstwhile life cascading in colors from black to brown to pink to red like a perverted rainbow. He parted his lips.

The Hotel Room

Something wet, stinking of mint and his mother's arthritis ointment, woke him. The prostitute was trailing her wet hair over his face.

"You're tired."

"When did I fall asleep?"

"Hour ago."

He went to the bathroom and closed the door. While one hand kept busy with the aim, the other rubbed sand from his eyes, an enormous amount for a short sleep but not unusual since his father's funeral.

"What were you dreamin' about?" The prostitute said through the door

"When?" He flushed the toilet and splashed cold water on his face.

"When you were sleepin'. Somethin' about hushsunni."

His father's warm, tobacco breath exhaled "hushsunni" into his ear. The sea gurgled at the base of his throat. In the mirror's reflection, he saw a long, white hair that had sprouted from his eyebrow. He examined it, curious when it had grown, for he didn't notice it this morning when he had gotten ready for work. He grabbed it between his thumb and forefinger and pulled, but it slipped through his fingers. He yanked at it again. Squawk! Zing went his head. The sea stormed up his throat.

"What about hushsunni?" she reminded him.

He choked back the sea. "No idea."

"I gotta go."

He took a step, but the floor heaved like someone had grabbed the edge and snapped it like a dirty rug. Deep breaths. Float. Float out of here!

He opened the door and floated past her to his wallet. Squawk! The sea foamed in his mouth. He grabbed some bills and shoved them at her. She took them and left. After shutting off the lights, he lay in bed with his eyes open; his heart banging away in the space of a cavern, beating to a mythology that strung from star to star across an enigmatic sky. It was there where he watched himself tumble into sleep.

In the morning, he woke to people talking and wheeling their luggage down the hallway. A pigeon cooed outside his window, and the sun sprayed between the dark curtains. Closing his eyes, he nestled his nose farther into the pillow and burped, bringing up the taste of last night's steak. The bend of wakefulness fell away.

He slumbered into a dream. The prostitute sat across from him smearing hollandaise sauce over her eyes and with mock panic mixed with laughter yelled, "I can't see! I can't see!" Embarrassed by her behavior, he tried to pry her from the booth, but she remained intractable, droplets of lemon butter tears rolling down her cheeks, "I can't see! I can't see!"

An oil painting on the restaurant's wall displayed his father's likeness. Silver hair rose like divine light out of the tenebrous background and within his narrow, pale face, eyes the color of glaciers watched him. But this was not his father. Not like this. Behind him, the waiter said, "Your steak, sir," and he turned from the portrait. The waiter held a plate on which a white hen sat squawking. He tried to push it away, but the old waiter proved too strong for him. He turned back to his father for help, but the portrait changed and now his father had closed eyes and a finger pressed against his lips. Not believing this was still his father, he searched for a nameplate on that ornate, wooden frame and found it at the bottom. It read "Hushsunni."

He woke from the dream unable to open his eyes, thinking the hollandaise sauce had caked on his eyelids, and struggled bewilderedly because the prostitute had smeared it over hers. Touching his fingers to his lashes, he felt sand. Relieved, he cleared away the pieces along with the fading squawks.

The Funeral

Four months ago, lilies surrounded his father's urn, an urn insufficient to contain his father's life now torched fingerprints, dental work, DNA – identifying markers of this single life lived, gone.

In the pew, he sat next to his mother on one side and his sister, her husband and their five-year-old son on the other. His mother clasped his hand during the priest's homily, and he, with his other hand, covered hers, which felt like the remains of a small, forgotten bird.

His sister leaned into his arm, and her little boy squirmed in his seat. He thought back to when he was that age. He often sat outside his father's office at home listening to him talk on the phone. Sometimes, his father invited him in and sat him on his lap. They would look at graphs of purple, red and green mountain ranges with peaks like broken windowpanes. "Just between us men," his father said. In the ashtray, a cigarette burned a smoke signal to the sky.

When his sister knocked on the locked office door and tried to open it, his father would tell her through the door to go help her mother. Although he thought this treatment of his sister unfair, those moments alone with his father were like inviolable filaments that wound around them both, encasing father and son together in a cocoon. When they emerged from the office, his father took him to the movies or the arcade or if it were August, the fair.

When he turned eight, those threads loosened, and his father no longer called him into his office. Business trips took his father away longer than they had before, and he, too, went on his own trajectory, but his father remained a stalwart presence, guiding him up and down mountains until he could do it himself. Yet, when his mother called to say his father had died, a cold wind ascended through him that left him blinking at the impartiality of death. He yearned at that moment for his father's direction. A direction he hadn't sought in years.

His mother slipped her hand out from between his when she stood to give the eulogy. He rose to accompany her, but she patted him on his chest, and he sat back down. As she talked about her husband and his philanthropy, he studied the life-size Jesus on the cross, his wan body, protruding ribs, doleful expression, the drops of blood from the crown of thorns and five wounds, a life forsaken. "Generous . . . magnanimous," his mother's voice trembled. His sister's hand trembled as she brought a tissue to her face. And the ephemeral blood of Jesus trembled offering nothing but a heart. He wanted to rip open that bear trap of a rib cage and steal the heart to give to his father whose own heart had failed him.

When the funeral service ended, he escorted his mother up the aisle and when they had reached the top, he looked back over his shoulder half-expecting to see his father's ghost standing behind the urn. Instead, he saw a white mother hen on the cross, wings outstretched, its slumped head wearing a crown of thorns, and on its body, a spot of blood like a cherry placed on snow.

The Birthday Party

"About time," the sister said.

"I showed."

"The cake's been cut."

"Who's that?" He nodded to the scene beyond the kitchen window.

"The clown."

"What's she doing?"

"Grabbing doo-doo out of her ass."

"Classy."

The clown threw the brown, plastic piece to squealing children. His nephew caught it.

"Kids love her. But, she's not cheap."

"What a racket."

"The clown or the kids?"

"Well, there you are." The mother put a ball of wrapping paper in the trash. "Do you want cake?"

"Hi, Mom." He bent down and kissed her cheek, smelling a trace of arthritis ointment, a reminder of that night at the hotel, the prostitute's wet hair, his dream, hushsunni. The floor stirred.

"Did you bring your nephew a present?"

He reached into his back pocket and took out an envelope.

"Oh, dear."

"Another savings bond. Why can't you get him a toy for once?"

"We all have to grow up sometime."

"He's six."

"See, it's already too late."

She hit him in the arm.

"Politeness, please."

The clown gave an end of a green ribbon to his nephew who pulled it while the clown sneezed out more green ribbon.

"I wish Dad could see his grandson grow up. He would've been proud of him. He always liked boys."

"Oh, he would've been proud just the same if you had had a girl."

"Maybe, but he was sexist."

"Stop speaking ill of the dead."

"But you, dear brother, were special. Dad never allowed me in his office."

"You weren't interested in his business."

"Is that how you remember it? Besides, he started bringing his grandson in his office last year."

"He did?" The sea whirled in his throat.

"Yes. Proof that he preferred boys."

166

"Now, stop. He loved the both of you equally."

"I doubt that."

His nephew wrapped the green ribbon around his body. He recalled again the times his father had invited him into his office and hoisted him up onto his lap. That feeling of specialness, the "just between us men" time. Swallow. Swallow hard that sea.

"Are you staying for dinner?"

"Can't. Meeting."

"Oh, for heaven's sake, what's that clown doing now?"

"She's pretending to expand the balloon with her gas."

His nephew jumped up and down and twirled in place.

"Oh, dear. He might get sick from all that spinning."

He thought back to when he fell ill to the ground after riding the tilt-a-whirl. His father carried him to the bathroom where he vomited into a toilet corn dog and pink cotton candy and in that kaleidoscope of food and acid, he saw a white mother hen. He had forgotten the origin of the hen until now, and his hand touched the white hair on his eyebrow.

"You're a million miles away."

"Thinking about my meeting."

"Let it go, son, and enjoy the afternoon."

Son. From the rim of that saturnine, low-slung sky, he watched himself in the bubble. Watched himself twist the white hair. Watched himself look at the sister cover the birthday cake; his mother wipe the counter.

"What did father do to you?" He watched himself look at the mother who stopped wiping and looked back at him.

"Nothing." From the sky, he pushed a finger against the tensile bubble.

"'Nothing' is the time of your meeting?"

"Now. It's now." His shoes sank into the stirring floor. Float! And, he did.

The Drive Home

He drove to his house in a milieu of fried and sugary foods, hay and dirt and organ music. His father's arm pressed against his in a tilt-a-whirl car and then his arm pressed against his father's. Back and forth, fast and faster it spun. From the sky, he reached down and stopped the tilt-a-whirl. Carnies smiled: saggy faces, missing teeth, greasy hair. He felt sorry for them and frightened that that might be his fate. They hadn't done anything, his little boy mind reasoned, to have to live like this. It was unfair. His father said not to feel sorry for them, for bad things happen to bad people. "Am I bad?" "No, son," his father replied, "You are loved."

He watched himself park in the driveway of his house and sit in the car. He watched him flip the memory over and back again like a coin and then bite down on it. When he removed the memory away from his mouth, he saw a crude, half-moon of teeth marks.

The Hotel Room

"Let me help you relax." She took off his shirt and pulled him closer, her tits scarcely registering on his chest. His breathing quickened when she reached into his underwear and wrapped her fingers around his cock and stroked it. "You like this?" He put a hand on top of her head and pushed her down to her knees. She pulled his pants and underwear down and enclosed the warm, wet hole of her mouth around him. He grabbed her by the hair and guided her head back and forth, slow, slow. He could feel the tip of her cold nose.

The sound of sucking made his blood pound in his veins like the hooves of feral horses galloping across a desert. He jerked her head back and forth, the horses gaining steam down those veins rushing, their muscles taut and luminous in the desert sun, kicking up sand that clung to sweaty bellies and legs. An image of his financial advisor's ass flashed in his mind. Back

168

and forth, fast and faster, desert sand sprayed, "what did dad do to you," horses skidding, sensing a cliff, halting hushsunni.

He yanked up his underwear and pants.

"What's wrong?"

His shoes sank in waves of nausea.

"Get out." A whisper thinning, thinning, thinning. Hushsunni.

From that lamentable sky, he watched him in the bubble sit down on the bed and take bills from his wallet. He watched him watch the prostitute leave.

The floor cockeyed, he grabbed onto furniture as he made his way to the mini bar and back. He sat down and waited for the squawk. None came. He brought his hand up to his eyebrow and felt for the long, white hair. It was gone. He drank one bottle followed by others on that bed floating through his softening consciousness.

He woke the next morning to a dry mouth and a headache. No noises from the hallway. No pigeon cooed outside the window. No sun pressed its way through a crack in the drapes. He ran a finger over his eyelashes. No sand. He got up and walked on a level floor to the bathroom and took a piss. After downing two glasses of water, he went to the nightstand, gathered his things and left.

The Park

He crossed the street from the hotel and cut through the park to get to his car. It began to drizzle, so he hunched his shoulders against the chill. A man lay supine on a bench, covered by smashed cardboard boxes. A soiled shoe stuck out at one end. He considered his own shoes. Bits of leaves and dirt stuck to the toes. A squirrel ran across the sidewalk and up a tree where he saw another man in tatterdemalion clothes leaning against it smoking a cigarette. The man laughed as if hiccupping and pointed a finger at him. The sidewalk cracked where a tree root had erupted from under it and he jumped over the tuberous offering and onto a level part of the sidewalk. His body shivered and drops hung from the ends of his hair and eyebrows. He wiped the rain away from his face and brushed against a long eyebrow hair. Squawk! Zing went his head. He stumbled off the sidewalk and ran through the grass, the swell of the sea breaking past his lips. Squawk! Squawk! Little fingers grab but keep slipping, daddy groans and guides his hand telling him to, "Hush sonny, and do what's right, sonny, it's sun, sun, sunny outside, gotta do what's right just between us men."

From a weary sky, he watched himself stop at a tree, rain twitching on the bubble like a swarm of amoebas. He reached through the branches and with his finger broke the bubble and all that contained within spilled forth and was swooped up by the white mother hen who herded those ill-forgotten pieces under her belly. Leaping down from the sky, he stood beside himself and placed an arm around his thundering, quaking shoulders.

A DEFINITION OF EVIL

By Mike Sherer

The little shits are out already. Beverly better be passing out the candy. Kids in this neighborhood get mean if they don't get their candy. Donald idled at the traffic light, fuming. A small dinosaur passed before him in the crosswalk. With the change of the light Donald raced toward home. Last year they killed the burning bush. Tore it to pieces. Beverly just laughed about it. "Shouldn't pass out suckers."

Turning onto his street, he nearly clipped a little harem girl. Her mother pulled her back, furious. "Slow down you son of a bitch! A lot of little kids are out walking in the dark tonight!" He glared at her, ready to yell back that it wasn't dark yet, when he saw that she, too, was in costume. Another harem girl. Whereas the costume looked cute on her dainty little daughter, on her it was sexy. Scant swaths of colorful flimsy material draped loosely about a nubile young woman, with only golden panties and bra underneath. Damn. Her little girl is going to do very well tonight. He grinned sheepishly at the pair, shrugged, then drove on down his street, much more slowly than before.

Just in time. As Donald pulled into his driveway he saw a mob of monsters assembled in the front yard. These were older kids, of questionable age to be trick or treating. They were all similarly outfitted, with no actual costumes or masks, merely ragged ripped clothes and painted ghoulish faces. And what faces. One had an eyeball pulled from its socket and dangling on the cheek below. One had a huge thick tongue that emerged from a gaping mouth and drooped down below its chin. One had a shaved head with a large spike embedded in a bloody hole on top of its skull.

Donald clambered quickly out of his car, not easily accomplished by his six-foot four, two-hundred and fifty pound frame. "I see I'm just in time. Hold on, I'll get you kids something. No suckers this year. We've got candy bars. Big ones." Donald rushed past them into the house. A bag of candy bars was sitting on a table just inside the door. He stepped back outside with a handful. One by one, six in all, the ghouls filed past him with open bags. Then filed silently away.

"Beverly!" Donald stormed into the house.

"Back here!"

He rushed to her call, which had come from the guest room. Where she sat hunched naked over her sewing machine. The dark-haired slip of a woman was at work on a small piece of shiny gold material, which contrasted sharply to the pale skin of her bare body. "Don't you know the little monsters are out already?"

"I can't come to the door. I've got to finish our costumes. You're supposed to pass out the candy."

"I got held up at the office. I tell you, the gang I just saw could have set fire to our house."

"Don't be silly."

"Our pumpkin was in peril."

"Did you light it?"

"TRICK OR TREAT!!"

Donald rushed back to the front door. Another large group had assembled on his porch, younger kids this time. He passed out candy bars to a pirate, a witch, a Batman, and a vampire. At the back of the group were the mother and daughter harem girls. As the young mother leaned over to help the little girl, her large tumbling tits nearly spilled out of their flimsy wraps. After she straightened, and Donald regained his breath, he

172

quickly spoke. "I'm sorry about earlier. You were right. I was driving too fast."

The young mother stared blankly back. "I don't know what you are talking about."

"Oh. You mean I didn't almost run over your daughter?" The pair hastened away. Seeing more kids approach, Donald rushed into the kitchen, opened the refrigerator, grabbed a beer, popped it open, chugged deeply, and then rushed back to the front door just as they arrived on the porch.

After two more large groups passed by, Donald had a chance to find some matches and go out to light their pumpkin. Beverly had carved it. She had done an expert job. She owned a set of pumpkin carving knives, and had taken classes. She took Halloween seriously. It was her favorite holiday. The parties, like the one they were going to later tonight, were her favorite ones of the year. She certainly enjoyed decorating the house. The malicious cat carved into the pumpkin was only part of it. There was also the murderous scarecrow in the front yard, the pile of leaves with the bloody arm emerging from it, the huge web with the gruesome spiders on the front porch. Those spider webs were everywhere. Beverly knew how much he hated spiders. So every year she strung fake webs up all over the house and filled them with all sorts of loathsome creatures. Donald stepped back to admire the glowing pumpkin. It looked so good, so hellish, he could practically hear its fiery howl.

The next hour was hectic. A parade of color and imagination. Donald passed out all his candy bars, resorted to money. He also drank several more beers. He turned on the news and glanced at it between runs to the door. A bad wreck on the Interstate. Real bad. A semi and some mangled metal which had been a car. And an overturned horse trailer. Traffic was completely stopped. There was a lot of blood on the pavement. Several bodies lying about. One in particular.

Someone had draped a sweater across the shoulders where the head should have been, only there wasn't a head, the sweater seemed to by lying flat upon the pavement, all there was beneath it was an explosion of red, of several different hues. A huge magnificent black stallion was tethered to the pick-up truck that had been towing the horse trailer. It was seemingly uninjured, and calm, considering it had been pulled from the wreckage. It placidly watched the hectic activity all around it. As if patiently awaiting its rider. Incongruously, in the midst of the carnage sat a carved pumpkin. Donald was called away at that point, and by the time he returned sports was on.

So he went for another beer. There was a loud banging at the front door just as he emerged from the kitchen. He opened the door to a towering Frankenstein, well over seven feet. "That's really a good costume. Fantastic. I mean it. Best Frankenstein I've ever seen. Stilts, huh? I bet it's really hard to walk, with those big clunky shoes on the ends of them. But I'm sorry, I'm all out of candy and cash. Just now ran out." Still the Frankenstein monster glowered menacingly. "Tell you what. You look like a big kid. Here. Have a real treat." Donald tossed the unopened can of beer into his bag. Frankenstein slowly turned and shuffled away. "Hey, don't tell anybody where that came from, okay?" The hulk stalked noiselessly off into the night. Donald stepped out to extinguish the pumpkin, cut off the porch light and close the door.

"Trick or treat is over," Donald proclaimed as he walked back to the guest room. "They cleaned us out." His wife was still bent over the sewing machine. He stopped, another beer in hand, just inside the door to study her nude form. "Aren't you cold?"

"Do I look cold?" she replied without pausing.

Donald stepped up to peer down over her shoulder. Still she didn't acknowledge him. So he pressed the beer can against one small puckered nipple. Beverly grew still, closing her eyes and sucking in a short breath. Her nipple stirred, then blossomed, as he rubbed the cold can across it. "Are you enjoying this?"

"Yes. Do the other one."

"You're weird." Donald stepped back and drank deeply.

Beverly opened her eyes and resumed working. "I told you we didn't have enough candy."

"Yeah, well, I passed out money, too."

"How much?"

"I don't know. I didn't count it."

"I bet it was more than another bag of candy would have cost."

"And a beer, too."

Beverly stopped working to look back over her shoulder. "You gave a can of beer away? To a kid?"

"Yeah. It was a big kid. Really big."

"I hope the police don't come looking for you tomorrow."

"Yeah. I guess that wasn't too smart. But hey, it's Halloween, the time to do stupid stuff." Beverly turned back to her sewing. "There was a hell of a wreck tonight on the Interstate. I saw it on the news. The Interstate was shut down. There was at least one fatality. Damn camera crew got out there before the ambulance. It was really bad..."

"TRICK OR TREAT!!"

"Shit. Have you got any money?"

'No. And don't give out any more beers."

Donald rushed to the door and turned the porch light back on. It was the ghouls again. He thought. Some of them looked the same. Like the one with the popped-out eyeball. There couldn't be too many of those walking around. Only there were more this time. A dozen? He stepped out onto the porch. "I'm sorry, kids, I'm all out. I had my light turned off. That means it's all gone. Sorry." They all remained still, staring at him. Half of them were out in the gloom of his front yard, merely dark forms, half were closer, within the glare of his porch light.

A near one caught his eye. A teenage girl with a zombie face wearing only a bloody filthy ripped tee shirt that hung loosely halfway to her knees. Through gaping tears and holes in the thin fabric her entrails were spilling out. Donald smiled at her. "Hey, that's a really good costume." She picked up her dangling intestine and offered it to him. Donald gagged, stepping back. "Damn. It even smells real." She shuffled forward, moaning and proffering body parts. Donald stumbled back to his open doorway. "I'm sorry," he called out one final time, then hurried back inside and slammed the door.

Donald turned off the porch light again. "Damn kids." He looked out through a small window set high in the door. He could see dark things wandering about his front yard. Her costume looked so real. Wonder if I should call an ambulance for her? Finally, he turned away and yelled down the hall. "What's for dinner, Bev?" Please don't say sausage.

"I didn't have time to fix dinner," she yelled back. "I have to finish these costumes. There will be plenty to eat at the party."

"But I'm starving now."

"Then fix yourself a sandwich. I'm busy."

"Then fix yourself a sandwich," Donald quietly mimicked as he walked into the kitchen. He produced a loaf of bread from the pantry, a knife from the silverware drawer, then went to the refrigerator for the mayo. Upon opening the meat drawer, the largest blackest hairiest ugliest most vicious spider he had ever seen sprang out at him. He screamed! Lunged back, launching what was in his hands all about the kitchen. The attacking spider struck him on the chest, then fell to the floor. He screamed again, scrambling backwards, around the table over a knocked-over chair up against the sink. He stared in horror at the monstrous spider. Which remained motionless on the floor.

"That was incredible." His naked wife stood in the kitchen doorway, phone in hand. "One more." She snapped a picture of him frozen up against the sink. "Now clean up your mess." She walked away.

Donald eased his white-knuckle grip upon the sink as his racing heart ever-so-slowly decelerated. His hands began trembling as he finally released the sink. It was then he noticed he was wet. He staggered across the kitchen, avoiding the so lifelike vileness on the floor. In the hallway he finally regained his voice. "Damn you, Bev! You made me piss my pants!"

She laughed loudly. "Don't blame me if you can't hold your beer."

"You know how much I hate spiders."

"Of course I do. Now clean up your mess. Both of them."

"Damn you," Donald cried out one last time as he waddled into the bathroom. He kicked off his shoes, pulled off his wet clothes. He scrubbed himself, rinsed, and dried. Leaving his filthy clothes on the bathroom floor, he walked out naked to the guest room. Beverly was once again seated at her sewing machine. "I'll get you back one of these years," he swore to her bare back.

"No you won't. You're not as ingenious as I am."

"You mean devious. Wicked. Evil."

"Yeah. Here." She stood, a bunch of shiny material in her grasp. "Are you clean?"

"Of course I'm clean. Do you want to inspect me?"

"Not now. Try it on."

He took the costume, laid it down in a flimsy pile, then held up one article - a pair of thin shiny gold panties. "They look awfully small."

"They're supposed to be small."

He awkwardly poked his large feet through the small elastic openings, tottering, on the brink of pitching forward onto his face. He pulled them up, yanked them up into place. He picked and tugged at them, cramming his genitals down in the front and trying to stretch the back up over his butt. "They're too small."

"Of course they are. Try on the rest of it."

He picked up the matching gold bra with the sewn-in breasts. He slipped his arms through the straps, then turned around for his wife to fasten it. "You mean I have to dress you, too?"

"I'm a lot better at taking these things off."

"No you're not. It takes you forever. There. Now turn around." He did, and she positioned his breasts.

Next he stepped into the gossamer harem pants. The rest of the costume, the veil and slippers and wig and jewelry, went on easily. While donning all this he continued talking. "I saw quite a few harem girls tonight. There were even two different sets of mother and daughter harem girls. I guess they were different. They acted like they were. But they sure looked the same. So this is a pretty common costume."

"How many men did you see dressed up as a harem girl?"

"Well, none, actually. And I didn't see any women dressed up as a sultan, either. Is your costume done?"

"Almost. There. Now let's go in the bathroom and put your make-up on." In the bathroom, "You left those disgusting clothes just lying on the floor? And I bet that mess is still in the kitchen."

"I'll clean it up while you finish your costume."

"Just do it before Al and Jill get here."

"What are they coming as?"

"I don't know. But you know how they like to play."

"Yeah. It should be a great party."

"Just remember, I've got a wicked scimitar. If I catch you flirting with any of the men at the party I'll cut your balls off."

"Bev, if I ever start flirting with men I'll cut my own balls off."

"That's it, Don. This is as much of a harem girl as you are ever going to look like."

Donald stepped back to gaze upon the completed image in the mirror. "Yeah. Isn't Halloween great?"

"Now clean up your messes." Beverly walked out of the bathroom.

Donald picked up his soiled clothes and carried them to the laundry room. Then he went to work in the kitchen. As he knelt on the floor to wash up the spilled mayo, the elastic of his panties bit into him no matter how much he pulled and tugged. Finally, he stood and, as a last touch, kicked the fake spider across the kitchen floor. Then he opened another beer.

"You are one sexy harem girl."

Donald turned to see a middle-age couple clad in concealing jackets standing in the kitchen doorway. "You better watch what you say, Al. Bev has a scimitar." He stepped up to take their jackets. "Has it turned that cold?"

"We didn't want to scandalize your neighbors," Al replied, removing his jacket. He was regaled in the full dress uniform of a German Nazi officer. Then he removed Jill's coat, which had been draped across her shoulders. She was wearing a short ragged peasant dress. Her hands were tied behind her back with elaborately-knotted rope.

"Wow, Jill. I'm going to be tugging at my panties all night trying to get them to fit right," Donald said as he piled the coats on a kitchen chair. "You two want a beer?"

"Sure," Al replied. Donald handed one to him, then hesitated before Jill. "You'll have to feed it to her," Al instructed. Donald opened the can and poured it into a glass. Al, adopting a loud stern German accent, declared, "And don't slobber the beer all over yourself!" With that he grabbed the back of her skirt and raised it with one hand, while with the other he yanked a black riding crop off his thick black leather belt. He struck her bare ass several times. Jill stood perfectly still and erect while being whipped. Al then released her skirt and replaced his riding crop. "Where's Beverly?" he asked, without the accent.

"She's in the guest room finishing up her costume." Al walked out. Donald turned his attention to Jill. "Didn't that hurt?"

"Yesss." Donald stepped behind her and lifted her skirt. Her bare bottom and the backs of her thighs are covered with red welts. "Don? Can I have some beer?"

"Sure." Donald released her skirt and held the glass up to her lips, letting her sip slowly. As she did, with his free hand he pulled the front of her dress out to look down at her breasts. "Has Al been beating on anything else?"

Tilting her head back from the glass, she replied, "Not yet."

Looking up, he smiled. "With your hands tied behind your back you are anyone's toy to play with."

"Yesss."

Releasing her dress, he gave her another sip of beer. "How was traffic? There was a hell of a wreck out on the Interstate."

"I didn't hear anything about a wreck."

"It looked really bad. There was this headless guy, and a big black horse, and a carved pumpkin..." Donald spilled the rest of the beer on Jill as they both jumped at the sudden racket on the front porch. He quickly set the glass down and rushed into the living room to throw open the front door. The porch was covered with broken eggs. "Damn punks! We've been egged!"

Donald stepped out onto the porch. He could not see anyone in the dark. But they were out there, he was sure, watching and laughing. The front picture window, the wall, the door were all running with slimy egg. Looking out into the dark shadows of his front yard, he bellowed in anger, "Damn punks!!"

The door slammed shut. Donald lunged for it. It was locked. He looked in through the small glass set high in the door. Beverly, Al and Jill were all looking back out at him, laughing. Beverly raised her phone and snapped a picture. "Dammit! Let me in!" They all laughed louder. Then one of them turned on the porch light.

Donald could hear the laughter, the jeering, from the darkness of his front yard. He pounded furiously on the door, screaming, "Let me in!! Let me in!!" He could hear more laughter from inside.

The first egg missed, but it struck the wall to the left of his face and splattered all over him. The second was wide, the third one struck him on the right shoulder. Enraged, he turned to confront his attackers. "I'm calling the police!!"

"Go ahead, pervert!" came back at him from out of the dark.

Donald turned back toward the door to beg to be let in again. His foot slipped in egg slime. He crashed hard. Slid across the porch. Into a spider web. The cottony web and several large ugly plastic spiders stuck to him. He thrashed about in the slimy egg, fake web and terrifying plastic.

The porch light went out and the front door flew open. Donald looked up to see Beverly, still naked, backlit in the open doorway. At her sudden appearance the eggs stopped flying. She was furious. "You better not have messed up that costume I worked so hard on!"

"Me? Me?"

"Get inside!"

Donald crawled and slid across the front porch back into the house. Beverly slammed the door behind him. Still on his hands and knees, Donald asked, "Who locked me out? Who turned the light on? So all the neighbors could see me like this? So those punks could egg me?"

The other three looked at each other, then burst out laughing. Al, with his hack German accent, declared, "I know nothing!" then gave Donald several hard pops across the butt with the riding crop. The laughter grew hysterical.

Snapping another picture with her phone, Beverly said, "This is going up on Facebook tonight."

Donald sat back on his haunches and, with egg running down him, with web and spiders in his hair, stared pathetically up at his wife. "Why are you so mean to me?"

Smiling wickedly, Beverly replied, "Because you love it."

"Come on, Don, don't turn sour now," Al said as he grabbed an arm and pulled him to his feet. "We're just bored middle-age people trying to amuse ourselves."

"Bored middle-age people trying to amuse themselves," Donald paraphrased. "That sounds like a pretty good definition of evil to me."

Al released his arm, then tried to wipe the egg from his own hands. "So now we're evil. Bev, get your husband another beer. He needs it bad."

"I don't have time. I have to finish my costume or we'll never make it to the party." Beverly walked out.

Al stared after Beverly as she rolled down the hall. Then he turned back to Donald. "Come on, Don, go get cleaned up. I'll get you a beer."

"I'll help you clean up," Jill offered, easily slipping her hands out of their bonds and laying the rope aside. "Hey. This one's moving." She flicked a rather large spider off Donald.

Donald stared dispassionately at it as it skittered away. Then, tugging at his panties, he followed Jill to the bathroom.

SHUFFLE

By James Pyne

Shuffle

They look at me through the barred window with their rodent faces. They're the prisoners even if they don't see it. They resent me because I'm free. I can think whatever I want. Do whatever I want. Be whatever I want. My life's a bunch of paintings and paper. I'm the creator of new worlds. I'm a poet some days. A full-blown writer other days. I'm shuffling pages and paintings all over the walls of my room, I'm all possessed-like; they tell a story that I must put together. I'm Mother Nature with a magic fountain pen.

Yes, this one. *The Man with the Golden Helmet* by Rembrandt, or whomever painted it. They say it's not his work. It doesn't matter. It belongs here with the story that's unfolding all over these walls. Most paintings have a page taped to the bottom of their frame with part of the story. And now I write another one.

Shuffle

Michael was the only angel remaining in the steaming desert that was Hell. Everyone else had *turned*.

He lumbered onward as the Flaming Cacti slowly advanced after him. His impregnable helmet and armour that had been beaten into shape by Hephaestus' art wasn't so impregnable here. The law of the universe, the rules he lived by, none of it meant anything in this forsaken place. He didn't dare take his helmet off even as much as his greying beard itched like crazy. He felt almost mortal, feeling pain, and his sight wasn't the best here.

"I know you can hear me," Michael said to the sky that was lit up in flames from the dragons burning the fleas off each other. "I'll find you and end this."

Michael hadn't been here long so his back was still paining from his wings being torn from them. Archangel Raphael's sole duty these days was to yank the wings from an angel's back before their descent to Hell. No one had yet left Hell to reclaim their wings. Not having wings meant something as harmless as walking Flaming Cacti were a problem in large numbers.

Michael wasn't sure how Big Cranky would take to his only son, Lucifer's, death, but Michael was feeling kind of betrayed right now. Tossed to Hell for questioning Big Cranky's motives for the universe. "*You get your kicks from all these tests you put mortals through, tempting them with things you damn well know they can't resist. What is the purpose of this madness? I swear, you've cracked.*" And to Hell Michael was banished at the snap of a finger.

The lava-fissured desert began shaking, opening up into a lake of bubbling magma that the Flaming Cacti splashed into, though they tried backing off to no avail. Michael steadied himself on a small fissured float of land as molten entity pushed out of the flaming lake that was three times the height of Michael. It took shape.

"Poseidon," Michael said, withdrawing his sword.

Poseidon, long ago cast to Hell, ruled over the lava pits like he had with the oceans of many planets. His once blue skin, now cracked with flowing lava, like the skin of every other fallen angel except Michael. That was something Michael wanted nothing to do with. But his skin was already ceasing to sweat, advancing signs that he, too, would crack if he didn't hurry up and find Lucifer.

Poseidon drifted toward him, the lake up to his knees.

"His trusty sidekick before me now," Poseidon said, arms folded. "Even you have fallen from His favor. Look at where following the rules has gotten you." Poseidon leaned over Michael. "I haven't forgotten it was you who put me here."

Shuffle

I thought about having Michael and Poseidon teaming up together and having Lucifer defeating them and chaining them together to a boulder with each getting their livers eaten by baby dragons. But that's the problem. You can't force this. You got to let it play out naturally. Any planning is interference with the natural order of things.

I shift paintings around on the wall. I'm obsessed. I'll spend hours rearranging the paintings and pages on all four walls, trying to figure out this universe I've discovered. The prisoners out there have ceased giving me new paintings, but they still give me paper. I'm like an experiment to them, an amusement so they can forget about their pathetic lives at home. They only make my resolve stronger. I shouldn't complain too much, they allow me this fountain pen, something the others in here don't get due to safety reasons for everyone involved. It's Dr. Michaels' own personal fountain pen, I might add. I have his blessing, his eye.

Yes, that's what's missing. I take the reprint of *The Birth of Venus* by Sandro Botticelli. I begin writing a page to go with it. It will continue Michael's initial meeting with Poseidon. I don't number the pages anymore because I'm forever shuffling them around, taping them to the frame of this painting, then that one, careful not to tear them, making it all fit. Each page is its own story. Sometimes just a paragraph, other times the entire page is crammed with the Printed Word. And so I write.

Shuffle

"You, of all the Fallen, know where Lucifer is," Michael said to Poseidon, leaning on the hilt of his sword. He was still on the fissured float of land within the newly created lake of lava flow.

Poseidon folded his arms, looking past Michael, as if he wasn't worthy of being looked down at. "I rather like this place. Why would I help you destroy it? Lucifer is no friend of mine, but we have a common enemy today that I shall squash." Magma creatures lifted from the lava, sitting on fiery seahorses that exhaled fire at Michael whose armor and shield protected him, for now. The flames scorched the bits of silver hair cascading from his helmet like firecrackers about to go off.

"Don't you want to go back home?" Michael shouted.

"Home? Everyone is in Hell now. There's no one to go to; Heaven is an empty place of broken dreams and ideals. Here, we are truly alive, free to do what whatever we want." Fireballs formed in his hand that he whipped down at Michael, almost sending him into the lava lake. "Why do you resist? You'll be one of us soon enough. Embrace it, Michael. Stop clinging to the old ways."

"I'll not become this place."

"Stubborn to the end, then."

The Magma Monsters on their fiery seahorses came at him from all sides. He slayed them one-by-one, sending halves of seahorses and Magma Monsters splashing back into the lava. Poseidon swatted Michael's shield into the burning lake. He kicked Michael down and now stomped him into the tiny piece of fissured float. His helmet now grossly dented.

Poseidon lifted him over his head. "Baptismal by fire, old friend. You'll thank me for this."

"Put him down," a familiar voice said, as flames plowed through the Magma Monsters and permanently turned them into ash and steam.

Michael was too weak from escaping Poseidon's grip, but had enough in him to turn his head to see Aphrodite hovering over the molten rock, her skin lava-fissured, her flaming hair spat out sparks, her eyes were pure coal.

"Put him down, Poseidon. Because believe me, I'm too hot to handle even for you."

Shuffle

They just gave me food. Some days I eat it. Some days I don't. It's all about the starving artist thing being their most creative when their belly is a steady rumble. I'm like Van Gogh here, maybe I should cut my ear off. Not both. I have no interest in outdoing Van Gogh to sate my ego. I can't of course dismember any part of my body, if I do that, the prisoners will take away my paintings and pages, or maybe leave them at the orders of Dr. Michaels. Maybe Dr. Michaels would order them to take away just my fountain pen, prompting me to desperately rearrange the pages, looking for an ending hidden somewhere in there that I'd never find. Only Dr. Michaels knew that was how to get to me. He understood me. He knows I'm always looking for that ending, that perfect ending. Is it so much to ask for?

Of course, there's another piece. I take the reprint of *The Lady of Shalott* by John William Waterhouse and hang it on the right of *The Birth of Venus*. Over two hundred reprints patching the once dull green walls, most in order now, with one page taped to each of their bottom frames. I begin writing another page.

Shuffle

Poseidon allowed Michael passage thanks to Aphrodite's interference. The lava-cracked desert began pulling itself back together as Poseidon sunk back into the earth, arms folded.

"I have one friend here, at least," Michael said, sheathing his sword.

"Friend-zoned so soon?" Aphrodite turned away from Michael, her hair was nothing but long strings of flames. "It's good to see you, too. But I'd hate to be the bearer of bad news, you can't stop it from happening. You'll look like us soon enough."

"Come with me and we'll free all angels from this damn place and return to our previous glory."

"Live a little." She turned back to him. "You're still following things by the book. Faithful Michael, even at the expense of his happiness." Aphrodite pressed her body against his, the warmth of her seething body heating his armor. Her coal eyes turned into orange embers. "Stay with me, and I'll help you get through the transition. Stop running away from…"

"So Lucifer has sent you to enchant me." He pushed by Aphrodite.

"He has done no such thing. I haven't even seen him since arriving here."

He ignored her, walking toward the flaming mountains along the horizon.

"You'll see I'm right," Aphrodite yelled behind him. "You're running away from the inevitable."

Shuffle

The painting *The Great Day of His Wrath* by John Martin has no story to go with it. Until now. I have never been so inspired. I'm in the zone. I can't remember when I last slept. Doesn't matter. Sleep is for the dead, like most of the people in his place. But these walls are alive with me.

Shuffle

Michael trudged through Hell, meeting old friends along the way. Some remembered him, others stared blankly at him. The lost, mad flaming eyes of Zeus as he randomly speared thunderbolts at volcanoes, crumbling them into rubble. The flaming mountains along the horizon were closer.

"I must ask you since you've just freshly arrived." Zeus leaned into Michael. "Do the mortals remember us?"

"They tell tales of us," Michael said, wanting to hold Zeus by the shoulders with his bare hand like old friends, but Zeus had long ago fissured with lava and wouldn't be friendly to his still-angelic skin. The gauntlets remained on. The helmet, too, because friend and foe were impossible to tell apart here.

"Do they sing songs about the glory of the First Angel War? How the Tentacle Terror and his Army of Monstrosities fell before our might? What of the last great war?" Zeus was referring to the one that led to the Great Flood.

"They just remember our names to further their personal gains, nothing more."

Zeus's flaming eyes closed. He turned away. Looked over his shoulder. "Good luck on your quest, Michael."

"You will not come, then?"

"I see no point, who will write of it?"

"We have a duty to the rest."

"The old ways are dead," Zeus said, turning away from Michael. "Our glory days have long past. If you ask me, settle down, have a family, make the best of it."

Zeus collapsed more volcanoes with thunderbolts as Michael reluctantly turned away from an old friend. They had seen many battles together. To see him like this, it was like Michael was seeing his own future.

Shuffle

I scotch-tape the page to the bottom frame of *The Great Day of His Wrath*, and leave it alone for now. Only a few more paintings without a story attached to them. So little time to successfully tell their present fate. There are no rewrites. Once printed on paper, that's it, on occasion there's a word crossed out here and there but there's only one draft for each painting. That's not a problem because it all comes out natural once I get started. I go into a trance and feel what they're feeling. Because they are living right now. We all imagine new worlds. New places. We're all deities.

Dali's *The Persistence of Memory* is next. The pages are being written in chronological order now. A good sign. I still don't know the ending. I don't dare guess it. I want to be surprised like Dr. Michaels will be. He has such an interest in art that's inspired by all this painted art around me.

Shuffle

"Step no closer," Hades said to Michael of an area that looked normal one second, the next, it was distorted, like looking out from behind a waterfall. Hades was gangly, hunched over, his body cracked with moving lava. His charcoal eyes widened as his arms began to droop, and then his upper body fell backward, struggling to rise back up. For him, walking more than a few steps was impossible.

"Wherever I go, things become affected like me." It was even difficult for him to talk for any length of time. "Just keep your distance." He looked at Michael from the point of someone dancing the limbo. "Do I know you?"

"It's Michael." Hades stared at him, seemingly clueless to the name. "What horrid act deserved your fate?"

"Lucifer fears competition for Hell, I imagine." The volcanoes and crimson-red boulders began drooping, almost like they were slowly dripping into oblivion. "It's becoming increasingly difficult to keep myself together." Hades tried erecting himself, his arms not cooperating as they sagged to three times their length. "Go the other way, stranger. In my space you'll continuously remember the bad memories, the regrets; and everything good you'll forget. There's someone I feel like I should remember, a female."

"Persephone," Michael said of Hades' wife.

"Who?" Hades looked up for a few seconds, then his neck bowed at the middle leading to the rest of him collapsing into a puddle in the shape of an elk horn. He slowly began gathering himself back together as Michael turned away for the fiery mountains. It pained Michael to see old friends in such states. Hades forgetting the one woman that unconditionally loved him. She could be standing right in front of him and he wouldn't know her. What cruel madness this place is.

Shuffle

Dr. Michaels will be here soon. And there were only two paintings left. I will surprise him. He'll be impressed. If only I could free him. He's the greatest prisoner here. Bound by words from books written by his profession. His religion. His barred mind.

The next painting is *Starry Night* by Van Gogh.

Shuffle

Athena walked down the spiraled steps leading down from a throne within the flaming mountains. Her gold armour withstanding the heat from the fissures of lava branching all over her skin. Her Medusa shield attached to the back of her armor. The formidable Athena, adopted by Lucifer after Zeus disowned her in fear she would overthrow him as he did his father.

"Keeping the throne warm for your father?" Michael clasped the hilt of his sheathed sword, just in case. He had finished her training after Lucifer had been banished here. Michael had done his best to be a father figure to her. But her daughterly love for Lucifer was no secret.

"I have not seen him." Her swords remained sheathed. That was a good sign she was not doing her father's bidding, that being to protect him at all cost.

"You lie. I understand your love for him, Athena, but look at all the suffering around you because of him."

"There's nowhere to go," Athena said. "You've already found him. All of us, including the volcanoes, the dragons, and other beasts, everything, are a part of Lucifer."

"You mock me."

"You don't see the obvious, Michael. It's right in front of you."

"All I see is *his* madness."

Athena turned from him, went back up the step. "You see what you want to see."

Shuffle

Dr. Michaels is hunched over as he finishes reading the ending.

"Brilliant," the doctor says, making notes.

He's a handsome man, wisdom-grey beard and thick-rimmed glasses. He's the only one who understands me. Or at least tries. I think he'd fully understand me if he'd just let go, for he's the biggest prisoner in here. But I'd be lying if I said I was totally free. I'm not. I'm a prisoner of love. It's Hell. This love. Because he can't return it because he's a prisoner of his books, of his teachings, of his peers who wouldn't smile kindly on such a relationship. But I see it in his eyes, he looks longer at certain parts of my body, and when he meets my eyes, he stares, briefly forgetting his prison.

"And this one," he says, holding the only painting without a page taped to the bottom of it. An untitled Zdzisław Beksiński reprint showing two people sitting, they're stricken by severe famine to the point of almost being skeletons, and in their horrific states they still hug each other lovingly tight. "An extra then? Ah, I see. The story's not done."

I say nothing, knowing I have a beaming smile going on.

"I'll get a new collection of paintings," he says. "And more paper, of course. A new pen, if you need?"

I'll free him one of these days. Through my writing, he'll see my mind, feel my heart beat for him, and he'll crack, too, and we'll finally be together.

Shuffle

AUTHOR BIOS:

Stories by **Maggie Veness** have appeared in several countries, in a range of eclectic literary journals and anthologies, including SLICE, Nazar, Bravado, Gem Street, Crime Spree, Skive, Best Lesbian Erotica, The Maynard, Adanna, Litro, and countless others. The majority of Maggie's work has been print published. She lives in NSW, Australia.

Jessica Bowden is a freelance writer and educator. Her passion for all things art inspires her daily pursuit to capture the mystery of life. A reader and lecturer by day and a writer by night, Jessica lives and breathes fiction. Find her on Twitter @Bowbowboom.

Catherine A. MacKenzie writes poems and short fiction most women can relate to. She writes all genres but usually veers toward the dark. She has been published in print and online publications and has self-published short story collections, books of poetry, and children's picture books. Cathy lives in Halifax, Nova Scotia. www.writingwicket.wordpress.com

DJ Tyrer is the person behind *Atlantean Publishing*, and has been published in *Sorcery & Sanctity: A Homage to Arthur Machen* (Hieroglyphics Press), *State of Horror: Illinois* (Charon Coin Press), and issues of *The Literary Commune*, *Tigershark* and *Carillon*, and has released a novella, *The Yellow House* (Dunhams Manor).

Essel Pratt is a master of horror and fantasy, conjuring tales that haunt souls and inspire imagination. As a student of psychology and teller of tales, Essel writes to share the complex nature of his imaginings with the world. His ever-expanding catalog of short stories spans multiple anthologies and collections, ranging from whimsical fantasy to bizarre horror, including everything in between. Dedicated fans have praised his creations, labeling his talents as prolific in substance.

Hailing from Misahwaka, Indiana, his passion for writing began in the early years as his imagination taunted from within, begging for a release. Dabbling in art at first, he found that the stories that pleaded to be told could not be imprisoned by ink and paint alone. His most notable and prevalent accomplishments include Final Reverie, Sharkantula, and the multiple short stories that have garnered a following of their own, such as the adventures of Detective Mansfield.

Inspired by C.S. Lewis, Clive Barker, Stephen King, Harper Lee, William Golding, and many more, Essel doesn't restrain his writings to straight horror, instead exploring the blurred boundaries of horror within its competing genres, mixing the elements into a literary stew.

Lance Hyden was born in the mean no, high-spirited streets of Detroit, Michigan. He traded the cold for heat by moving to Phoenix, Arizona during high school. After being stationed in California while serving in the Marine Corp, Lance moved back to Michigan and graduated from Eastern Michigan University with a degree in film. Finding the sun more attractive than the snow, Lance moved back to Arizona where he lives with his wife and their four boys.

After years of considering himself a writer, **Paul Rhodes** decided that it was time to stop scribbling on beer mats and cocktail napkins and get serious. His short stories "Blind Man's Bluff" and "The Man Above" have appeared in past FTB Press anthologies. He lives in Faversham, England, with his wife, Faye, and son, Dylan.

Phil Richardson writes speculative fiction, horror, mystery, and literary fiction often with a humorous bent. He is retired from Ohio University where he met his wife in a creative writing class. He has published two collections of short stories: *Little Bits of Out There,* and *Little Bits of Darkness,* and over 80 stories online and in print including 30 in anthologies. Two of his stories were nominated for the Pushcart Prize. His website, PhilRichardsonStories.com, has links to many of his stories.

A fiction writer and essayist, **Sandi Sonnenfeld** is author of the memoir, This Is How I Speak (Impassio Press), for which she was named a 2002 Celebration Author by the Pacific Northwest Booksellers Association, which recognizes writers whose work merits special notice. Her work has appeared in more than two dozen literary magazines and anthologies, including *Sojourner, Voices West, Hayden's Ferry Review, ACM, Raven Chronicles, Necessary Fiction, Perigee,* and *The Doctor TJ Eckleburg Review* among others. A graduate of Mount Holyoke College, Sandi holds an MFA in Fiction Writing from the University of Washington, where she won the Loren D. Milliman Writing Fellowship. For more, visit www.authorsandisonnenfeld.com.

Na'amah Segal is a writer, communication coach, conduit, nerd, and mother of two. She loves to write, embraces the power of stories, and her spiritual purpose motivates everything she does. She loves helping others realize their potential and hopes to complete her first novel in 2017.

Stephen McQuiggan liked nothing more than walking under ladders, breaking mirrors, and taunting magpies until he fell into a sudden and inexplicable coma. His first novel, *A Pig's View Of Heaven*, is available now from Grinning Skull Press.

Bryn Fortey has been active on the British short story and poetry scenes for more years than he cares to remember. The Alchemy Press published his debut collection, MERRY-GO-ROUND, in 2014

Rob Nicholson was born in 1969 in Detroit, Mi. Schooling at Southfield Senior High School, Specs Howard & Eastern Michigan University. Currently living in Tempe, AZ with his wife & teenage son. His favorite author is Stephen King.

Frank Roger was born in 1957 in Ghent, Belgium. His first story appeared in 1975. Since then his stories appear in an increasing number of languages in all sorts of magazines and anthologies, and since 2000, story collections are published, also in various languages. Apart from fiction, he also produces collages and graphic work in a surrealist and satirical tradition. They have appeared in various magazines and books. His work is a blend of genres and styles that can best be described as "frankrogerism", an approach of which he is the main representative.

By now he has a few hundred short stories to his credit, published in more than 40 languages. In 2012 a story collection in English ("The Burning Woman and Other Stories") was published by Evertype (www.evertype.com). Find out more at www.frankroger.be .

Chris Moylan is an Associate Prof. of English at NYIT where he publishes short fiction, poetry and literary criticism. He is the author of Border Taxi (Abaton 2010), a collection of short fiction and travel poetry set in the Middle East, where he taught for several semesters.

Jill Boyles' work has appeared in *Toasted Cheese, The Ilanot Review*, and *Calliope Magazine*, among other publications. She holds an MFA and was the recipient of a Minnesota State Arts Board grant and a finalist for the Jerome Grant. She's currently working on a novel. Her Web site is jillboyles.com.

Mike Sherer's screenplay was made into a movie titled 'Hamal_18' and was released direct to DVD in 2004. The film can be located on IMDb. Mike's blog, 'flanging' can be found at mikesherer.wordpress.com. Currently, Mike is writing short stories and working towards finding a publisher for his recent novel "A Cold Dish."

James Pyne was born in New Glasgow, Nova Scotia. His writing is forthcoming in the *Ugly Babies 3* anthology. He's currently working on the completion of his latest novels, *Woe* and *Big Cranky*.

Other books from FTB Press:

Irrational fears can be described as an anxiety or phobia of seemingly normal or innocuous objects, animals or happenings. The fear can be subtle or paralyzing, either way it makes for a great story. This is a collection of those stories. Irrational Fears is an anthology of works from a talented and diverse group of international writers.

ODDisms is an attempt to find meaning in an undefined word. The stories are of strange beliefs and practices which take the characters into oddball situations. Everyone has their quirks, what happens when the quirks become your philosophy or belief systems? Let's find out. Some of the ODDisms include Escapeism, Thirdism, Uberism, Chimerism, Refitism, Gethinism, Ambi-Americanism, Hackism, and Tuneism. These are just a few of the –isms that attempt to define ODDism.

Russell Greenbeaux is a clown and he's running for president. His oddball campaign takes off when his message about political dysfunction inside the Beltway catches on. Along the way, his campaign encounters challenges from evil lobbyists, an angry reporter, an odd assortment of third party candidates with obscure agendas, covert infiltration from the major parties, Republicans waiting to be raptured, Democrats who invent mind control technology to win the culture war, and a murder mystery.